Visceral

Stories of Obsession, Desire, and Decay

Jessica Joy

© 2025 Jessica Joy

All rights reserved.

This is a work of fiction.

Cover design by Rebecca Robinson.

This collection contains themes and subject matter which some readers may find disturbing. Please refer to the end of the book for more details of content warnings.

What's New, Kitty Kat?

I would kill Enzo four days after his 52nd birthday. He would be the most surprised of all. Even that didn't account for the smile on his face.

But that's jumping ahead. Kitty sits, stiff-legged in the faded armchair, and stares down at him. Enzo kneels at her feet, ignoring the strain in his tendons and the pain in his left buttock. Rain drums its fingernails against the tiny casement window.

'Hold still, Cherub.'

He pushes the rolled-up stocking onto Kitty's unforgiving foot. It slides up her smooth, tanned leg. Over the years, suspender clasps have become tedious, so he turns the nylon into a tornado twist and tucks it into itself. Like Nanna used to do.

On the side table, the ticks of the small enamel travel clock echo in the silent room.

Enzo's metal hand catches on the upholstery and pulls out a single red thread. He unhooks his metal part and smooths over the small loop of cotton.

After dragging the other stocking off his shoulder, he inches his thumbs down inside to the toe; his fingers are mandibles that scrunch and ruche the sheer fabric. He's careful not to catch the carbon fibre fingers of his prosthetic on the fine weave.

Kitty's second foot is frozen in a point. Arched, balletic. He eases the stocking to her thigh, twists it and tucks it in.

He pulls her skirt down over the knotted nylons. Sighs. When he looks up into her wide, green eyes, she's looking to the side, exasperated.

'I know, Kitty Kat, but as we've discussed, tights do not cater for your very special requirements. Now, hold your elbow still while I make some adjustments to the hinge.'

From behind the privet, I watch Enzo close his front door, using the key in the lock. He's careful to quieten the ke-clunk that would otherwise shake the house. Nanna couldn't abide slammed doors.

As he scuttles towards the bus stop, the large briefcase drags his left side down. I think it's caused by years of wearing a prosthetic arm that's always been a bit too heavy for him. The new aluminium and carbon one came after the damage was done. He moves the briefcase to his right side and flexes the fingers of his false hand.

Poor Darling. Rumour has it that the absent limb kept him alive. Somehow. After his small plane went down during a trip to Vietnam, he was missing in the jungle for three months. He was only nineteen then, always such a slight man. The arm was probably crushed in the crash.

Probably.

I wasn't there. But, as I've heard him tell Kitty on several occasions, "What happened in U Minh, stays in U Minh." Anyway, he's a vegetarian now.

When I dream about Enzo, he's always a small boy with blond curls and a cheeky smile. I'm searching for that little fair-haired boy, in my dream – not the man version. The 'man' Enzo is huge and hirsute; incongruous. In real life. And, of course, I don't know him. At all. Only what I've observed.

Last night I dreamt about him, but as a knee-height man. He had a weird squeaky voice that turned my stomach. I wanted to get away from him. But he clung to my leg, his bionic hand embedded in my flesh. I tried and tried to shake him loose, but he had so many bionic limbs, and they all grabbed me and pinched my skin. I woke up screaming, 'Let me go!'

Balanced on an upturned milk crate, I peep into the living room at the back of his bungalow. The window box has a shallow layer of dried earth and a few dead stalks. Everything important to Enzo is indoors.

Kitty sits straight-backed in the old leather chair. My father always sat in a chair exactly like that every evening, his dinner on a wooden tray with glass bead handles. He'd stay there to watch the 10 o'clock news, the tray on the floor, slid underneath the chair. That's where we found him on that cold, mizzle morning, face contorted as if the news had annoyed him to death. Stiff like Kitty.

I don't bother watching Kitty for long anymore. She's boring. I'll take a slow walk to the hospital.

Inside the hospital, armed with a bag of grapes, I can wander for hours unnoticed. I can even sit in the waiting area of Orthotics and Prosthetics and watch Enzo at work. Watch him say goodbye to his patients. He gives them a lollypop if it's a child and watches them until they turn the corner at the end of the corridor. He will give a little finger wave with his metal fingers. The child looks back. Always. They will smile. Or wave back.

It might be all the grey that leaves me unnoticed. Grey hair, grey coat, grey skin. I am like a haze, a shadow, a mist of unremarkable.

If it stays dry, Enzo will take his sandwich outside and sit in the Garden of Peace. From my hiding place behind the great oak, I love to see him feed the pigeons. He is kind.

Tonight, he'll be off to the Thomas Theatre Players, at the Teddy Thomas Centre. At the centre you can do pottery classes, holiday French, flower arranging; lots of activities for crowds of people, who move around the centre hugging yoga mats and music scores. Amongst them, clutching a notebook, I am anonymous. Hidden at the back of the balcony where they store the old props and costumes, I can watch the Players rehearse, unseen, unchallenged. Tickety boo.

The balcony is covered in dust. The costumes reek of old sweat and cheesy feet. The wooden crate is crammed with false legs and articulated arms: donations from Enzo. He's not an actor, he's their make-up artist, and a very good one too.

I already knew that from looking at Kitty.

***

'I don't want to talk about it.'

Enzo sounds upset.

He sloughs off his coat and leaves it on the hall floor, a shed skin. In the kitchen, he flicks the kettle on. Then, with a grunt, he stomps back into the hall and hangs his coat up on the hook. His Nanna would be turning in her grave.

In the living room, Kitty looks expectant, so he plants a perfunctory kiss on her cheek. 'I'm sorry, dear. Hello. How was your evening? Let's have a cup of tea before I get you ready for bed, shall we?'

Her cheek still glistens with the moisture of his kiss.

Once the China teacups have been placed upside down on the draining board, Enzo cradles Kitty and walks her across to the bedroom. While she's perched on the edge of the bed, he removes her clothes, lifting them carefully over her smooth curls. He folds each item, and places it neatly on the pink, damask chair.

He feeds one arm of the nightshirt along her articulated arm. It reminds him of a game he played at Scouts. A twisted wire was fixed between two posts, connected to an electric buzzer. The challenge was to move a metal ring along the convoluted wire without touching it. If you set off the buzzer, you had to go back and start again.

Things had not gone well at the Players' planning meeting.

'Yes, of course I showed them my Moby Dick pantomime script!'

BZZZZZ! The cotton catches on an exposed bolthead in her elbow. Enzo eases the fabric out and starts again.

Kitty looks worried.

'No, they didn't want to see my comedy, "Get Your Leg Over!"

BZZZZZ! The cuff is stuck on her thumb. Enzo pulls it round, and the sleeve slides to her shoulder. 'Apparently, farce is a no-no.'

When the front is buttoned up, he rolls down the pyjama bottoms and pushes her feet through, one at a time. He's tired and disgruntled, and he's rushing their bedtime routine.

'Yes, I suggested Richard III, again!'

BZZZZZ! The elastic in the waistband wedges into the mechanism of her knee. 'For Pete's sake!' Enzo tugs hard, and the tiny wires snap.

He buries his head in her lap and weeps: big, snotty sobs of frustration. Kitty falls forward and rests her head on the back of his, until he's cried it all out.

After he's dried his face and blown his nose, Enzo pushes the exposed sharp ends out of the way, pulls up her pyjamas, and settles Kitty on the pillow.

'I'll get the solder iron out in the morning. It's an easy fix. Tickety boo.' He pulls the sheet up to her chin and kisses her forehead. 'Night, night, Kitty. I love you.'

***

The more invisible I become, the bolder I feel. It's seven in the morning. The bag of cat treats rustles in my pocket as the paperboy cycles past, catching me sneaking through Enzo's side gate. I start calling, 'Pusskins, come on, Pusskins,' and I rattle the bag of kibble.

The boy doesn't look back.

It's Enzo's birthday. I'm balanced on a planter like a roosting chicken, under their bedroom window. Their headboard is right under the sill. All I can see are the hillocks of their feet under the mustard-yellow throw. A candlewick throw, like my mother's. Through the open window, I focus on Enzo's voice as he winds up the alarm clock.

'In my dream, I was so small and scared (click, click, click.) And my mum is there. Not Nanna, but Mum, before she left. Well, no, she's leaving. She's always leaving in my dream (click, click, click.) I can't see her face. I never see her face, because she's so tall, so far up and away. And I cling to her, to the top of her leg (click, click, click.) But I can't keep grip. Her skirt is coarse and scratchy on my face and arms, and I can't hold on (click, click, click.) And then she pulls away, and she's running down the road, but I can't see her through my tears. She's gone.' (click click click click.) It was a stupid idea, coming out this early. I need a cup of tea and a sit down. I'll come back later, when he's cheered up.

I've already posted his birthday gift. The brass flap on his door snapped down so hard I thought it would wake him up.

Two tickets to Peter Pan at The Beckett. He won't take Kitty. If I can figure out what to say to him by then, maybe that second ticket could be...

I'll come back when the champagne's on ice.

***

From under their bed, I watch Enzo's bionic hand scrabbling at Kitty's stocking like a spider stuck in the bath. In the silence, I can hear the gentle whir of his mechanics, the rasp of silicone on nylon.

The carpet is busy and tacky. I have dust bunnies in my hair and something sticky on my elbow. Probably spilt tea. Probably. Well, I'm stuck here now.

His face is so close to mine. I can smell the mint of his freshly brushed teeth. The sour note of alcohol. And his sweat: organic, musk. He doesn't use deodorant. I've been through his things.

I want to smell the shampoo in his hair from under a fluffy towel.

Enzo surprised me by coming home early. He crashed around in the kitchen and opened the second bottle of champagne this week. I heard him dance Kitty round the living room in great galumphing steps.

The springs sink onto my head as Enzo climbs into bed. I turn my head to the side. He's a big man now, rather overweight. I clasp my hand over my mouth and keep my breaths shallow; an insect caught on a web.

When he talks, it makes me jump.

'You were right, Kitty Kat, you were right. My dedication to the group and my skill has, at last, been acknowledged. Head of Make-up and Prosthetics for the Thomas Players.'

He slurs and giggles after a hiccup.

'And, as a committee member, I can ask, nay, insist, that they at least read my script: "Moby Dick or Captain Ahab is Legless." Damn right, it's hilarious, Kitty, damn right!'

The bed springs creak and whine as he turns over, the underside brushing my shoulder. The bedside light flicks off, and I hear the smacking of inebriated lips as Enzo kisses Kitty.

'I love you, Kitty Kat.'

'I love you, too,' I say aloud.

***

I'm a stupid old woman. If I'd realised, I would have moved sooner. Done something sooner. But the gasp and the weird guttural sounds and the bed moving...I thought...I'm ashamed of what I thought. And when it went quiet, I didn't know how to come out from under the bed. What to say?

'Hello, Enzo. It's me, your mum. Sorry. Sorry I left. Sorry it's been so long.'

So, I waited, quiet as a moth. I listened to the tap of the elder on his window. I thought it was his breathing I could hear, his heartbeat in my ears.

He was already dead. My little boy. My big boy. Grey. Like me. And clammy. But with his arms wrapped round Kitty Kat and the biggest smile on his face. That cheeky smile.

I couldn't leave Kitty there. She's so beautifully constructed. Imagine what the local paper would do with that, imagine the headlines.

No. I'll look after her now, I'll take care of her. Make a better job of it this time.

We'll get along just tickety boo.

Mightier

She was woken from her slumber by the clatter of the lamplighter's ladder. The lighter puffed and muttered, and the wood creaked under his weight.

Easing herself from the crumpled sheets, she winced at the pain in her thighs. Her coins lay scattered on the floor.

The gentleman grunted in his sleep, and she waited for him to settle, keeping still as a gravestone.

How could a man who wrote such beautiful words, inflict so many bruises?

He'd followed the dirty tracks of her tears and sketched the letters on her flesh with his privileged finger. "Thou art more lovely than a peach..."

She moved to the window and twitched the curtain, allowing a shard of smog-veiled sun to throw light across the ornate box on the table. After turning the key, she opened the lid. There, in a velvet-lined compartment, lay his solid, gold pen. It was heavier than she expected.

The pen with which he had written tender and fond emotions.

The pen that had inscribed 'whore' across her skin as she begged for mercy.

On the mantel stood his mother's vase. The dried stems of long-dead roses gathered dust. On tiptoe, she reached into the vase and retrieved the bottle of laudanum. He slept deeply, thanks to a few drops in his drink. She crept to his side and applied some more to his slack, lascivious lips.

Then she slipped the knife from the sheath under his pillow. The tip was razor sharp. She knew this, for she had felt its kiss against her neck as he yanked her hair and whispered threats with his stinking breath.

Carefully, she etched the letters into his forehead with the end of the blade, copying the letters from her own skin. She'd studied the scarred shapes for weeks in the looking glass, watching them fade from Peony red to Oleander pink.

He stirred and snorted. She waited and listened to the blood rushing through her ears, and mopped his head with the tenderness of a nursing mother. Satisfied with her letters, she shook the pen over the wounds, letting ink seep into the cuts.

After pulling a shawl over her hair, she disappeared, like a ghost, into the street.

Now, whether he raised his hat like a gentleman or kept it on and risked insult, everyone would know him for what he was.

'Whore'.

Buried Alive

Don't panic.

It's a bit late for that. Pounding heart. Ringing ears. Dry mouth.

I can't believe I fell asleep. Who falls asleep in a coffin? What sick, twisted delinquent gets comfy on a tiny, satin pillow?

I did tell the doc I could fall asleep on a washing line. Cosy as a corpse in a casket. Although I'm not dead. Not yet.

I stretch my fingers and stroke the soft, silky lining. It's a lovely coffin. Not that I'm an expert. This is my first. Definitely wood. It smells like oak, I think. Smooth fabric. No padding, though; my arse is numb already. And I prefer two pillows. I'll have a crick in my neck in the morning. Oh Christ.

I need one of those little bells the Victorians buried with their dead, for just such an occasion. Bloody good idea. Although, if I'm in the city cemetery, you'd be hard pushed to have a conversation over the traffic noise, let alone hear a tiny brass bell under six feet of clay.

Better still, I need some handy grave robbers. They're in for a nasty surprise. I'm skint. Worse than skint, I'm "in debt" and not the maxed-out-on-credit-cards kind. I'm in debt to Tommy. And trust me, you do not want to owe Tommy Cornwell.

But I digress from slowly suffocating. I need a piss. How long can I hold it? Should I even bother? I'm so fricking hot in this Chippy suit. Sweat is pooling in my ears. Maybe I can shimmy my arms up and get the head piece off.

The debt? Gambling. It's a bit of a sad story. Or maybe you've played cards with me? Fleeced me. You wouldn't have lost. The thing with poker is, it's not about the cards. It's strategy and bluff and tells. I'm shit at it. But I always think I'm going to get better. I get great cards, and I think, this is it, this time I have to win. And then I fuck it all up.

It's like my life, really.

I finally fall in love and then fuck it all up by dying.

Ah, CC. She wouldn't marry me, but a bloke like me has to take what he can get.

CC said marriage was like when you finally get the doll you always wanted for Christmas. All the time you played with it at your friend's house, it was magical. Special. The hair smelled of your friend's place. She had all the clothes, the cot, and the hairbrush. You couldn't wait to go and visit again, so you could beg to play with her doll.

Christmas comes, and when you rip off the wrapping paper, your fingers slide over the cellophane window in the box, and there she is in her pink chiffon. You rip back the cardboard and inhale the chemical, plastic smell of new doll.

She has that greasy sheen to her hair. Her wrists and ankles are bondage-tied to the inlay with those interminably long bag-twists. She's all new and shiny and fake. But you realise it wasn't the doll you wanted.

It was your friend's mum. Your friend's bedroom. Your friend's life.

So, then the disappointment drags down the sides of your mouth as hard as you try to smile. Your mum says, 'That's the one you wanted, isn't it, sweetie?' There's that little knot of anxiety between her eyebrows.

And you say, 'Yeah, Mum, she's the one. She's perfect.' And you hug the cold sharp edges of the doll to you and realise it's not the first lie you've told your mum. And after that, lying gets easier.

I'd forgotten CC was talking about marriage.

'What happened to the doll?' I'd asked her.

'Oh, I cut her hair off and gave her tattoos with a felt pen. Mum whacked me and sent me to bed without tea. She threw the doll away. Stupid really 'cos I played with her loads more after she became a goth doll. I changed her into something I wanted.'

I nodded.

'See? Marriage. It only works if you can change the person into something you want them to be.'

I said, 'Shouldn't you marry someone because they're already something you want?'

'I thought I wanted my friend's doll.'

CC says she's cursed with perpetual disappointment. That's why she sets her expectations so low, no offense.

'None taken,' I'd said.

'Let's fuck,' she said, because she knows what she wants, and I respect that. I need that.

The first time, she'd been stalking me at Forestland. Every shift I did, she was there, in the queue for photos with Chippy. She looked incredible. CC is a living doll. She's tiny, and paper thin. Her style is Manga, and she looks incredible in short, pleated skirts and over-the-knee white socks (I never knew what Manga was, but CC looks like every picture she has shown me, right down to the big black eyes and blunt-cut bob. Although it's a wig. Her natural hair is long.)

That day, she loitered until the end of my shift and started to follow me as I headed to the staff exit. They're supposed to be secret doors, invisible to the public, but the public aren't as stupid as the corporation thinks.

I came out of character and told her I was sorry, but she couldn't come in the staff area. She said that was very presumptuous of me and winked. I thought maybe I'd misunderstood her double-entendre and turned to leave. She grabbed my arse through the costume. So, I let her through the door.

There's an old lock-up where you can get a little peace and quiet. I took her there. I was so nervous. I faked a fumble with the Velcro behind my head, delaying the inevitable.

'No, leave it on,' she said. I couldn't believe my luck.

'You wanna...leave it on?'

'Oh yeah,' she said, and her voice had that gravelly sound I've only ever heard on the porn channel.

I was too excited. I tried to picture Mrs Carnegie from primary school, you know, to slow things down. My hands were clammy and shaking so much, I couldn't grip the seams at the back of my costume.

'Wait,' she said.

I knew it. I sighed, thinking, here it comes.

But CC held up a pointed, white-handled instrument. She held it right up to the gauze window of Chippy's mouth, where I look out from. It had a sharp hook at the end with a little blob of red plastic on the point. There was a blade in the bend of the hook. It looked vicious. It looked dangerous. It looked like the sort of tool that should be nowhere in the vicinity of two people about to fuck.

Shit, I thought, she's a psycho. Of course she's a psycho, you absolute fricking idiot. I scrambled to my feet, knocking over a metal watering can. The costume is unforgiving in enclosed spaces.

'What the fuck is that?'

'Calm down. Come back here. It's just a seam ripper. For cutting through stitches. Look, we can cut a hole in the front seam of Chippy so you can...you know, stay in character.' She fast-blinked those big, dark eyes.

CC is a little bit genius and little bit terrifying.

So, I trusted her. I let her insert the seam ripper, and with a deftness I found strangely arousing, she severed the tiny stitches at my crotch.

'Okay. No talking now. Be Chippy, Chippy.'

The show was over in seconds. I hadn't had real sex in years.

I stayed in character, though, and clasped her miniature fingers between my big furry paws. I shook her hand, with Chippy's signature head wiggle. *Thank you.*

She handed me the seam ripper. 'Keep that handy,' she said with a grin.

I miss CC like it's been years, not hours. My feet are numb, but also the backs of my heels hurt. I wonder if I'll be conscious long enough to get bed sores. To notice them. The silence really is deafening. A high-pitched whistle fills my head, along with rushing sounds like waves on a shore. In different circumstances it might be quite soothing. I wish CC was here. Well, I don't, but she'd know what to say. She'd have a plan or some advice.

I love listening to CC. I know she talks to me like I'm one of her clients. Her dead clients. CC says she'd rather I didn't talk when I'm in costume. That's cool. I'm used to that. She's so deep. So thoughtful Some might say opinionated, but that's refreshing for me. I never know what to think. She says she gets a lot of practice airing her views to the dead. And since they don't answer back, she can change her mind, U-turn, reverse and reconsider.

All without judgement. It's liberating, she says, and it gives her space to think.

Funny, because I remember saying that to the boss at my interview for Forestland.

'How will you feel about having to put on a costume every day, not speaking, and having your body hidden and disguised?'

It will be liberating, I'd said. It would be nice not to be judged for the way I look.

He had the good grace to blush as he shuffled his papers.

'Okay, then. Well, you passed all the other tests, so, you can start out as Chippy the Chipmunk, and we'll review your progress in six months' time.'

That was seven years ago.

My arms have gone dead now. I can rotate my wrists and my ankles a bit. Maybe I'll die sooner of an embolism. A clot from lack of circulation. Or boredom. I wonder if I'll die of boredom before dehydration. How will I know if I'm delirious?

Maybe I'll finally get to talk to dead people. Like CC. Well, they talk to her. She says it's quite useful in her line of work. For getting their thoughts on that final outfit and make-up.

It's comforting to think I'll be able to convey my last wishes to CC. Although, I don't have any that I can think of. And of course, I'm already in my final resting place. No makeover for me. No sewn-shut lips or cotton wool cheek implants. No manicure, pedicure, or clay-assisted reconstruction.

I have a perfectly good suit in my wardrobe. Given the choice, I wouldn't have been interred in my work uniform; buried alive as Chippy the Chipmunk. Am I already dead?

'CC, can you hear me?'

I wonder if she's missed me yet. Has anyone?

At work, they'll be checking the rota. Has anyone seen Chippy?

I don't think Buffo, Racky or Podge know my real name, either.

It's not like Chippy to be late. (I'm never late.) Did he phone in sick? Did anyone listen to the messages yet?

Then they'll call me. Or HR will. Or my manager. Hope froths in my chest like an ice cream float. My phone!

But even as I pat down my concealed pockets, I remember CC tossing it on the steel tray with the suture kit and clamps. Sometimes, we screwed on the prep gurney. Don't knock it till you've tried it. We'd smoked something this time, and then the frills and cushion in the coffin had looked so inviting. CC went to get us a drink.

She probably thinks I left.

It was her lunch break. And soon, the funeral home will have a spare body and a missing coffin. I wonder if she'll work it out.

I only pulled the lid down because of my insomnia. I like it dark. And quiet. And drugged.

I imagine work calling me, and CC and her boss, Mr Fenwick, watching the phone for a moment as it vibrates between the scalpels and saws. I imagine Mr Fenwick's frown of compassion as he answers the phone and says, in that special quiet voice he reserves for the newly bereaved, 'I'm terribly sorry to be the one to tell you this, but I'm afraid the owner of this phone is now deceased. Please accept our deepest condolences from Fenwick and Black Family Funeral Services: making your last journey one to remember.'

Mr Fenwick never misses an opportunity to rustle up business. 'One thing in life is certain...' he doesn't finish the platitude, but leaves it hanging in the air, limp, ineffectual and damp. Much like his handshake.

He'll put the phone in his desk drawer and then he'll wash his hands. Again. He won't like the crack on the screen, or the rim of dirt, the smear of fingerprints and the dogs-arse smell of it. He's obsessive about dirt and stuff.

So great. At least work will already think I'm dead. They can start the paperwork.

***

God, this darkness is solid. It's pressed against my face and sitting on my chest. I'm used to looking at the world through the hazy gauze window in my costume, but this blackness is impenetrable. Intense. There's more light in space. I keep looking for stars. I hope I don't forget what CC looks like before I die. I'm going to lie here and just remember her for a bit.

Something in my other pocket is digging into my thigh, and I have to work it out with tiny scrapes and nudges. The seam ripper. I hold it to my chest for a while, like a crucifix.

How long has it been? I should try to escape. Claw my way through panels of polished oak until my fingernails hang off in ribbons. Then I could add excruciating pain to the myriad things that could kill me in here.

I'm going to unpick the satin lining. Or rip it. Just for something to do.

That's why I joined the card game. For something to do. People don't often invite me to things, so I'd jumped at the chance. Turns out there are three games running at the park.

My least favourite is in the changing area of the security officers' shower room. The security guys ripped out the benches and set up a table. It's cramped and still smells of old socks even though it's been out of use since they built the new block behind the admin building a couple of years ago. Painted, slimy white walls lined with metal lockers seem to loom over every game, and the constant drip of the shower heads make for a headache before the booze and weed would get going. The security guys cheat and then fight. They play dirty and they fight dirty. It's all the steroids. I only join their game if I'm desperate.

Then there's the game in the Hygiene Rec Room in Zone 3 (Cutieland – it's the toddler zone). The game only runs on weekends. The hygiene supe disapproves of gambling, drinking and sex before marriage. He's the son of a vicar and a son of a bitch if he finds a game going. But he doesn't work weekends.

Usually.

The cleaners have a well-stocked and well-hidden bar; the vending machine is kept topped up, and the refectory tables push together easily. Congenial lighting and good air-con make for a pleasant game. The cleaners are amenable to visitors, and they don't cheat.

Mostly.

But my favourite table is in maintenance, in what they call the Boneyard. It's a warehouse nestled behind 'Wildworld' where most of the height-restricted rides are. We sit in abandoned ride cars and upturned teacups, in amongst the grease and dirt. I once played a whole night on the back of a carousel elephant. We've played in ghost train cars, Ferris wheel buckets and sitting on cogs the size of tractor wheels. Bottles, cans and fag butts cover the floor, but every couple of weeks, Jackson brings the mini digger in, and we take it in turns to clear up. After a race with the FLT or the quad bike.

Jackson. I should hate him. He was the one who set me up with Tommy. Probably got a cut for it. But at the time, Jackson was so – concerned. He made it out like he was doing me a favour letting me in on the great big secret that was Tommy Cornwell and his bottomless pit of money.

Tommy had slid the inch of crisp tenners across the desktop, lining the edges up perpendicular to the gold border of the leather inlay. Tommy is so particular. The green paper band that hugs the bunch of notes even matches the leather of the desk.

His "office" is on the fifth floor of the old bank building in Swan Street. The lift is off limits. By the time you've climbed five storeys, you've reached his stained oak door (I knew I knew the smell) a hot, sweaty, out-of-breath mess. That's what he wants. To rush you. To keep you at a disadvantage, your nerves jangling, your heart racing. But not me. I spend hours on my feet in a fur suit. I thrive on hot, sweaty, and breathless. I know it irks him, too. He gets a twitch in the corner of his left eye.

I stared at the wodge of notes, my hands in my lap. It reminded me of Pass the Parcel, that tension of waiting for the newspaper-covered package to come within reasonable reaching distance. The fine-tuned timing of taking it from your neighbour as it passes the invisible border between your touching knees. The hair's breadth slowing of your movements as you pull the package into your territory. The greasy smear of ink on your fingers, the powdery, acetate spice of newsprint lingering in the air. You know you should pass it on, but you hold on to it for a fraction too long.

I reached across the scuffed green leather for the bundle, my fingers resting on the paper-cut edges. And I willed the music to stop. I was on a precipice. I could push the wodge back to Tommy and tell him I'd changed my mind. Maybe go down the traditional route. Get a bank loan. Apply for a new credit card.

I'd never be able to pay him back. This would end in pain.

I grabbed the money. Relief and elation washed over me, rinsing away the underlying nerves and dread. There was a game that night. I'd win the first payment. I had to.

Bill and Ben (the flowerpot men) saw me to the door. Two brick shithouses, they shadow Tommy like a couple of Rottweilers. I've never heard them speak. Their real names are Lofty and John. I don't know which one is which. For big men, they are surprisingly agile and fast. But they never indulge in unnecessary bullying. I respect that.

'Bill. Ben.' I nodded my farewells to them both. The taller one has a tell. His top lip quivers into the start of an Elvis sneer. It's like tapping the glass of a shark tank. I checked the bulge in my inside pocket and invoked Lady Luck.

***

I still haven't made the first payment. I've been dodging Bill and Ben for two days. Granted, that's the least of my worries, but it still niggles.

Jesus, my breath stinks. All I can taste is onion. And fart. That can't be good. I must have re-breathed the air in this coffin a million times. I'm gradually turning all the oxygen into carbon dioxide. I may start to hallucinate soon. Or is that nitrogen? I'm probably thinking of deep-sea diving. Easy mistake. Wouldn't normally catch me doing either. That great expanse of black water above and around you. Like layers and layers of earth. Yeah. No thanks.

Yesterday, CC and I had sex without the costume. For the first time. Was it yesterday? How long have I even been in this thing?

It's hard to judge. I'm good at endurance. I can wait hours before I need to piss. Or have a drink. It goes with the job. Stamina and discomfort. It goes with my life.

I remember the first time she saw me as me and not Chippy. We'd booked ourselves a cheap hotel room. Cc was sitting on the edge of the bed, her feet dangling. I'd taken off the head section, blowing my hair out of my face before looking down.

'Oh my god,' she said, and my heart plummeted to my feet. 'I thought you'd be blond.' She chuckled, that warm-hearted, throaty laugh that's way too deep for the size of her bones. She didn't flinch. She didn't baulk. She never mentioned it. I think I fell in love with her there and then.

'What about this?' I pointed at the port wine stain that covers the whole right side of my face. I don't do elephants in rooms.

'It's a beautiful colour,' she said. 'Must have been a good year.' She grinned. She wasn't deflecting. She meant it.

'I thought you'd want to cover me up with that dead peoples' pan stick?' I didn't want her to, but I wondered if it had crossed her mind.

She said, 'I don't make over dead people for dead people. I do it for the living. So they don't have to face their fears, their prejudices. Some people just can't picture the dead how they used to be when they were alive. Some people are too terrified of being confronted with their own mortality. I just make the dead more presentable for a tough crowd.'

And I remembered something my stepdad said to me when I came home with a split lip on my first day at secondary school. 'Tough crowd, huh? Maybe keep your hood up?'

CC stroked my birthmark. It was a feather touch, gentle. But I shuddered. I couldn't help it. No one touches my face. My mum did. And numerous medics. Oh, and Lucy Cartwright in the third year. For a bet, I'd found out too late.

'Oh my god, are you crying?'

'No. I have a tear duct thing.'

I wiped my eye. The room was so silent, I could hear the graze of my fingertips over my leathery skin. The rasp reverberated through my skull.

And it's the truth. I do have a tear duct thing. As if the birthmark isn't enough, I have a damaged tear duct, a lot of thickened tissue on my lips, and a subsequent speech impediment. Yep. Card dead. Great poker term for a shit hand. And no, it doesn't make me a better player because I know the lingo. It makes me a twat.

When I managed to look CC in the eyes, I saw she had teared up too.

'Oh my god, are you crying?' I didn't know if I should hug her. I told you: I am such a twat.

***

I could try to sleep for a bit. "I'll sleep when I'm dead." Good. That's my earworm sorted for – ever. 'Let's talk of graves, of worms, and epitaphs." Thanks for that, CC. Here we go then, the slippery slope into madness.

I stink. This costume had been smuggled out of the park months ago. I shouldn't be wearing it. Company policy. No items of/or related to park costumes must leave the park. Instant dismissal. It smells musty and sweet. Like sex and old pizza. What I wouldn't give for a pizza now. It's a bit sad to think that I've eaten my last one. I'd have enjoyed it more and paid attention to the toppings – probably pepperoni – if I'd known.

My ears are playing tricks on me because I hear a creak and snap of sheared wood and wrenched hinges. There's a hiss of stale air, and I squint into the sudden bright light.

'Jesus!'

'You called?'

My saviour is – Tommy. He looms over me, the twitch in his eye dancing. The silk lining I've unpicked flaps onto his shoulder, and I'm quite impressed with how much I've managed to free. Tommy's cigar breath fills my face, and he flashes his death mask grin. I notice a shred of something green wedged around his incisor.

'You still owe me thirty-four grand, sunshine.'

He's upped the interest. Again. His voice echoes, and I stare past him into a long, stone-built chamber. Fake candles flicker on the walls in imitation sconces. The walls drip and glisten in the candlelight. Coffin-sized recesses line the walls, filled with coffins in varying states of decay. The air is cold and stale; damp tinged with an earthy mushroom smell. I'm in a crypt. I'm in a coffin at the centre of a crypt.

CC. She's worked out where I am. If Tommy has touched her, I'll...

Tommy grabs me by the fun-fur at my neck and heaves me to a sitting position. I can't feel my feet yet, and my body screams with the sudden movement, but my busy hands and arms are buzzing with energy.

I've spent the last, who knows how many hours or days, basking in the relief of never having to see Tommy again. I even smirked to myself at the thought of him popping a blood vessel when he realised he was never getting his money back.

Despair consumes me as I stare into the huge blackheads between his eyebrows. I'd escaped all this. I was free at last.

I'm still gripping the seam ripper. In one swift motion, I plunge it into his temple. It finds the sweet spot, and his eyeball bulges a little as he lets out a surprised gasp. The ripper sticks out of his head when I let go of the handle, and it shimmers in the candle flames. Then I smack it home as hard as I can. He grunts. The other eye rolls back into his head, and Tommy falls forward onto me. We collapse back into the coffin so hard, my teeth clack together.

I lie still and wait for the scream of anger, and the rain of punches, and the thunder of his rage.

Tommy rears back up, and I cover my head with my arms, but his head lolls forward, one popping eyeball fixed on me in surprise. Bill and Ben hold an arm each.

'Is he...?'

A cold, wet dribble of something courses down my cheek, and I taste the coppery tang of Tommy's blood.

The two big men lay him on the flagstones and check his neck for a pulse. I couldn't hear a heartbeat if I wanted to; my head is filled with the percussion and whoosh of my own.

Ben shakes his head. Tommy is beyond help.

'Fuck!'

I grip the side of the coffin, sitting up like a bizarre vampire victim in a thirties film.

I'm in big trouble.

An unreadable look passes between Bill and Ben. They stand up, brush off their knees, and straighten their wristwatches.

I'm dead. It's merely a matter of semantics now. Long and slow death, properly buried alive, probably in agony from various broken bones and internal bleeding. Or a quick gunshot and back in the box. One can hope.

Bill and Ben grab me out of the casket. My legs are jelly, and my feet tingle and throb as the pins and needles pulsate through my toes.

'Gents, Gents. Lofty, John, how about...' I can't even begin to defend myself. A slow death it is, then. Here's hoping I pass out.

They sit me down on the cold step in front of the door. If I can just get the feeling back in my legs, I might be able to make a run for it. The door creaks behind me, buffeted by the wind. I'm hyperventilating.

They go to their boss. With the slightest exhalation of breath, they lift him by his shoulders and ankles and heave his body into the coffin. Bill takes the spotted hankie from Tommy's top pocket and mops up the bloodstain on the floor. Then tucks it back in the pocket, still dripping.

'Not a word.' Ben directs this at me. When he speaks, he sounds normal, like a mate or a colleague.

I stagger to my feet. They press down the lid of the coffin, making good a few splinters. Then they lift it between them into the nearest recess.

Bill walks past me and pulls open the mausoleum door. It's dark outside, and I can see a twinkle of frost on the yew. The night sky is mottled with yellow snow clouds.

'Mind how you go,' Bill says, and he sounds normal, too.

I step out into the cold night, and my breath plumes into the darkness. I take huge gulps of icy air. I'm alive.

Alive and debt free.

My watch says 7:45. Time enough to get to the Boneyard table.

The Restoration Man

His hands look like his mother's. He has her swollen joints and bulbous fingertips. But not clumsy. Never clumsy. Always careful and neat. She taught him how to sew. She taught him how to push the needle through with a thimble, keeping the edges close. How to be patient. Small, tight stitches. Baby steps, for baby feet.

No haute couture for Crockett, though. No tailor's dummy, yards of velvet or pinking-shears. But skins and pelts, carpet thread and leather needles, whip stitches and beady false eyes.

The candle-light gutters. Crockett stretches out his back and neck. With a sigh of satisfaction, he flexes stiff fingers. He hiccups a bubble of anticipation. This is surely his finest work – his piece de resistance.

It's a private project, commissioned through clandestine meetings in smoky snugs. A lady of means was desirous of his services; her grief had consumed her. No questions asked, he could name his price.

With furtive glances, the little body was passed to him swaddled in a blanket, hidden in a basket. A white silk gown and bonnet folded neatly and placed atop. And the tiniest mittens he had ever seen. He was quite envious of the craftsmanship.

Outside, snow has drifted at the shop doors across the street. Hooded windows peer at him in the yellow glow of the snow-covered road. Her ladyship's man will arrive soon.

He inspects the piece. His needlework is almost invisible, the seams – seamless. And he has left his signature on the pad of the foot; a tattoo of his cursive initial. On its back, a dead C. He chuckles.

Eyes open or shut, he'd asked. Closed, of course, in peaceful repose. So, the lady might nurse the little pet on her lap, still. Her friends and callers will be duped into thinking the beloved thing is still alive. They will swoon at the elegance of the trick. Crockett swells with pride at the thought of his workmanship fooling the rich and landed gentry. Oh, the commissions and repairs that will be asked of him. He shall need to keep a ledger. Possibly take on an apprentice.

There's a perfunctory knock at the shop door. Crocket removes his leather apron and spits on his hands to smooth his hair. He straightens his cravat and takes up the basket.

At the door, the manservant appraises him. Most certainly curious about Crockett's tools and methods, nay, even in awe. The wind gusts in, and he smells of stew and tobacco.

"I've come to collect Mr Ping-Pong."

He's all business, not a twitch of the mouth or crease at the lips.

Crockett hands over the basket. The manservant elicits a tiny gasp.

"Most life-like, is it not? Quite shocking to the untrained eye." Crockett smiles, benevolent towards the poor imbecile.

"Her Ladyship will most certainly be...surprised."

"Tell her Ladyship..." In a moment of inspiration, which he clutches at like a thread about to slip through a needle, he says, "...that 'The Restoration Man' is forever at her service."

The manservant inclines his understanding and then with the smallest shake of his head (the sign of a man struck dumb in wonder) he moves off into the blustery night.

Crockett closes the door and is consumed with a warm feeling as if he had just inhaled too deeply over the ethanol. The future looks as bright as a glass eye in gaslight.

Talking In Tongues

The twins twitch and chirp and squeak. Their fingers flap and flutter. Full lips and tongues pout and flick, and the room is filled with alien clicks and pops, and human laughter.

Angel watches them. Her sisters. They snap and crackle and suck, and savour every guttural sound their long, pink tongues can utter. They sip and swill; vintners sampling their own secret language.

The two girls sense her gaze. They turn to look at her with slow blinks. Their blue eyes dim, clouds gathering on a summer's day.

Angel looks back down at her book.

Tiggy and Frog switch to stealth mode. Hand signals only.

I'm going to lick her face. (Giggle.)

Well, I'm going to kick her face. (Giggle together, high five.)

The giggles morph into weird, throaty laughs. They mimic Angel's laugh. Not that she often has cause to laugh now. Not like she used to when they were small and cuddly and fun. Back in the commune, when Diana trusted her.

Back in the cult. *Let's call it what it was, Angel.*

Diana. Not Mother, or Mum, or Mama. Mama would have been so easy for Angel to say, to sound normal. To disguise the cavernous hole where a tongue should be. Diana told her she was born without a tongue so she couldn't tell anyone about her wings. Diana said that's the burden an angel carries – silence.

A sharp smell of disinfectant creeps under the door, into the ward. In the corridor the housekeeper mops the floors with eye-watering concoctions.

Angel picks at the callous on her palm. The one on the mound of her ring finger. The Mount of Appollo. The four mounds on her palm are raised and yellowed, each with its own rough fingerprint. She raises the edge of Appollo with her fingernail and pulls off a sliver of hard, white skin. Flakes of scalp, discs of dried-up blister, cuticles. So many spare bits of skin. And yet, when they offered to make her a new tongue, it was from her own flesh – to be carved from her thigh. Like a Sunday roast. She'd thought they'd collect up all the spare bits she'd shed and pack them into a mould. A tongue-shaped mould. Not gouge another gaping hole into her.

On the dazzling white wall, the clock ticks long, incessant clacks that beat out the interminable hours on the ward.

Clack

Same white wall with a footprint at knee height. Size 6 trainer. Angel's size, but not her print. She knows this because she lifted her foot and fit her own trainer over the mark on the wall. For a moment, they were conjoined. Twinned. Although her institution-issue shoes have a different tread.

Clack

Same vinyl covered chairs pressed up against the walls. Salmon pink, not hot pink. With small pock marks from the last chewing gum removal. Every week, Harris comes round with a palette knife and a bucket. He tuts and scrapes. Tuts and scrapes. The balls of gum plop into the bucket. Polka dot stains cover the grimy fabric.

Clack

Same reinforced windows looking out onto manicured grass, hemmed in with box tree bushes and wood chip verges. Surrounded by the twenty-foot-high, mesh steel fence. A fence that's as effective as Diana at keeping them all in. They've been taken from one prison to another.

Clack

Same nurse in mauve overalls with a huge bunch of keys bouncing off her hip. Big, solid hips that strain her trouser seams to their limits. Angel listens to the rhythm of the nurse's rubbing thighs, swish, swish, swish. The sound of a leather belt through the air. The sound before a slap to the face. The sound of a scythe slicing through derision.

Clack

Same sound as the clock in the Big Hall, where they bent their heads in silent prayer. For hours. In repentance. And silence.

***

Overhead, the buzzing strip light fills Angel's head with a swarm of angry bees. It's so hot on the ward. Her cheeks burn, and her armpits smell of cooked onions. The institute pyjamas have someone else's sweat sealed into the seams, the kind that no amount of washing removes.

On that overcast afternoon, Tiggy and Frog had been given a few minutes to gather up their things. Angel had watched them from the back seat of the police van. Before they were bundled into the social worker's car, tear-stained faces and sagging shoulders, they turned to her.

Fuck you, killer, they signed. Which confirmed they knew she understood every private chirrup and whistle, every wiggle and bend of their fingers. She made a heart shape with her hands. The plastic ties dug into her wrists. The twins had spat on the gravel and crawled into the back of the SUV. Angel settles into the short, upright sofa. The glow of the afternoon sun spills through the blinds, the shards striped across her outstretched legs. She closes her eyes and drifts. In her dreams, she relives her admission to the hospital. Goosebumps prickle on her arms as the orderlies help her out of the cotton slip.

The washed-out continent of blood stains disappears into the crumpled pile of her old life. She stands shaking, unable to focus on the gentle whispers and instructions. Behind her, the doctor says, 'Oh.'

It's not even a gasp – more a statement.

'How did you get these, Angel?'

The doctor hands her the tablet. But she can't type because the keypad is so tiny. Her big fingers punch several keys at a time so that nonsense appears on the screen. She can feel the doctor's breath on her back as she gets in close to examine the long stripes of scars. 'So, these are your wings.'

Angel squeezes her elbows so the doctor can see how the lashes spread over her shoulders and down her arms. Long, leathery flight feathers of skin.

'They're actually quite beautiful,' she says.

In her dream, Angel turns around, and it's Diana standing there, tracing the lines of her scars. Diana brings her finger up to her lips. 'Shhhh.'

Angel wakes with a start.

'How are you doing today, Angel?' The mauve nurse smells of cocoa butter and cigarettes.

Angel gives her the thumbs up and a tight smile.

'You can use your words with me,' she says. She means well.

But Angel understands the power of words. She watched Diana wield words like a sword, or a hammer, or a blanket, or a gag. Angel rations her own words. She's careful not to waste them where it will gain her pity or condescension.

Or disbelief.

She'd tried to tell the Gibsons. So many times. As head of the cult, Diana did not tolerate dissenters. The Gibsons had been there right from the start, helping Diana build it up. Helping her set the boundaries. Not laws or policies. Boundaries.

Then the Gibsons overstepped the boundaries. Angel had liked playing with Tanya Gibson. Angel tried to warn them: Skye, Tanya's mother and Rob. And then, one morning, they were gone. Fled into the night. Or so she was told.

Later, on her sixteenth birthday, she found and read all Diana's journals and drank a whole bottle of stolen Jack Daniels. In those flamboyant, swirling texts, she read the truth about what Diana had done to the Gibsons. With the Gibsons. To keep the 'commune' safe.

After the Gibsons, Diana directed her paranoia at the twins. Angel found Diana mixing rat poison into the twins' supper. Diana ranted about them being possessed, talking in tongues, saving their souls. Angel realised, with some satisfaction, that she could keep her sisters safe. Diana had taught her well. Angel would remind her of that, in the garden, from the blunt end of the pitchfork.

The nurse waits, with her eyebrows raised.

'Okay,' Angel says. Simple letters that almost sound normal. Almost. Movements that split the sores in the corners of her mouth. She licks them and tastes the metallic tang.

'Okay.' The nurse bites her tongue. She shakes her head a fraction, and walks towards the nurse station, her polyester-clad thighs scything the air. Swish, swish.

Angel loiters in the doorway as the mind doctor walks past in the corridor. He flicks through a buff file as though he doesn't want to see what's in there. Is it hers? He stops to huddle over the file with the man in the bowtie. They whisper about healed scar tissue at the base of the tongue. And trauma. And torture. Who are they discussing?

She looks back into the room at the other women on the ward, at their greasy hair and worn-down slippers. Her sisters sit in the window seat, cuddled like toddlers. They stroke each other's faces. They look happy.

In their session, the mind doctor picks at Angel's experience like she picks at her callouses. He worries a little piece until he can lift it up enough to stare at the raw wound beneath.

'What makes you think your sisters hate you, Angel?'
I killed their mother
'I don't mind if you write on the tablet, but I can't help you unless you tell me what you are feeling.'
Nothing. I feel nothing.

Always in My Heart

Why do the birds start so early? she thinks. Outside the window, a blackbird has launched into an incessant trilling. It's getting hard to keep track of the days, because she can no longer mark them off on the calendar. Strange, the little things she misses. Picking up a pen. Making a cup of tea. Going to the loo.

She has a sense of her shape. Of her height. Of her position, now, on the dresser. But, consumed with her own thoughts and ramblings, she's lost track of time. Forgotten how many days have passed. Or weeks. Or months.

The dining room curtains aren't closed, and a shard of sunlight slices the room in two. She sees the shadow of next door's cat as it sits on the windowsill and cleans itself methodically.

She fancies she can smell bacon cooking, but it's just her imagination. The sun has that lazy Sunday, morning glow to it, that lends itself to a breakfast tray in bed and a book. She misses reading, too. And coffee, although she is not hungry or thirsty.

There's a sharp rap on the front door. The heavy lion's-head knocker shakes the wooden frame, and the cat jumps off the sill with a yowl. Muscle memory takes over, and she feels herself walk across the threadbare carpet, kicking back the corner of the rug that has flipped over. She brushes her hand on the gloss of the door frame and notices the temperature drop in the dark hallway. She might see an outline through the stained glass at the top of the door. Auburn hair, slender shoulders, an impatient jig.

The caller raps again, two sharp knocks now they have the measure of the lion's head, the pressure needed, the shock of its impact dissipated.

She hears footsteps receding down the path.

Time contracts and expands as the shadows in the room lengthen and bend.

The room is in darkness.

There's a hiss as the pressure changes. A door has opened. Or a window. She hears whispers. Then the beam of a torch dances on the carpet, followed by two figures in dark clothes.

"There's no one in the bedroom."

"I told you the place was empty."

"Stop yapping and nab what you can."

"Got a laptop and car keys. What about the telly?"

"Leave it, it's fixed to the wall. Have a look in the drawers."

A man is standing in front of her. He leans in and squints. With both hands, he grasps her from the dresser. The movement is sudden and exhilarating like a roller coaster ride. Like being lifted and spun round by her father. Like being a child again.

She feels her contents shift and settle when she is tucked under his arm. He walks with her. Through the fabric of his coat, the hard edge of his phone glances off her curves.

They're in the hallway. Below her, on the glass table, is an old coffee cup ring, and a magazine folded open at the astrology page. The doormat is covered in envelopes and flyers.

The man sets her down on the table while he fiddles with the door. It sticks. She thinks, *you need to kick the base*. He places the torch under his chin while he struggles with the lock, and the beam of light plays on her edges and illuminates the mirror.

Oh. Her reflection shows her rounded edges and tapered base, her patent black finish, her shiny engraved lid, and her silver plaque.

'Always in my heart,' it says, in reverse, followed by some dates.

She's whisked off the table and through the front door into the cold night air. The ashes shift sideways. And she wishes she could remember whose heart she is in. Always.

Strange Honeymoon

The Big Top billowed and flapped in the gusts of cool evening air, and Harriet wiped the sawdust off her boots. She balanced on each leg and rubbed her toes against her calves. Then she peered through the gap in the tarpaulin curtain. The tent was hot and humid already, filled with the earthy, acrid odours of sweat and animal dung. She scanned the audience. Hats, bonnets, red shiny faces, teeth and hands, babies on laps, children on shoulders; bodies were crammed in tight and spilled into the aisles and outer ring. Dust motes floated up into the tent's apex, searching for space amongst the ropes.

A glint of metal in the back row caught Harriet's attention. A hip flask raised to whiskered lips belonging to Royston Harper. Her husband had found her.

Tiny fingers slid into Harriet's palm and grasped her thumb. Harriet bent down to Tilly and straightened the bows on her pink, satin dress. Tilly stood still while Harriet pulled a comb out of her pocket and brushed the child's long strands of beard and sideburns.

She left the curls; the wardrobe mistress had pinned them with matching ribbons. Harriet could hear the slow tick-tick of Tilly's clockwork. She combed the long, thick hair on Tilly's arms and brushed her ankles, so the locks rested on her shoes like hairy spats. The comb caught in a small mat of hair, like the ones she'd washed out after Tilly was beaten and kicked and left to die in a greasy side-street.

Harriet had grown up knowing about the clockwork people, of course. Her father was a watchmaker surgeon, after all. Whenever a clockwork arrived at their house, her father had whisked them outside to his workshop. Harriet helped. She watched and learned.

She passed him tools and parts. He answered all her questions. She'd told him daily she was going to be a great watchmaker surgeon, too. When her father betrothed her to Royston Harper, the betrayal had stung. Her father had bigger plans for her, he'd said, the chance of a better life.

The night she'd found Tilly, Harriet was on the run from that better life. The cogs and wheels of circumstance had clicked into place like a well-oiled machine. Disguised in her husband's long coat and top hat, Harriet sneaked to her father's workshop. It was her first time being back there since they'd argued. Since her marriage. Since her father's funeral.

There, she hoped to find a bag she'd hidden before the wedding, along with her late father's savings (not that there was much left). Under the coat, the slashed skin on her back stuck to her undershirt. But the pain of Royston's words cut deeper. *You belong to me now.*

Back on the street, she clutched a leather bag under her arm, her shoulder skimming the buildings as she clung to the shadows. Crossing a gap between the houses, she heard a whimper. She found Tilly curled up like a ball of rags. Her eyes were swollen shut, and her hair was wet with blood. She'd clutched a miniscule cog so tightly it had broken the skin, and blood seeped into the fur of her wrist. Her chest was split, and her clockwork had been laid bare. Springs and sprockets spilled out of her in a metal waterfall.

Harriet scooped up the panting child and rushed back to the workshop. She felt sure Tilly would die there, in her arms. The child opened her hand to reveal the simple cog, one Harriet had seen in every drawer of her father's workshop, one that was common in any watch.

And Harriet knew what to do. She laid the little body out on her father's workbench and pulled back the torn fabric of the child's pinafore. With trembling fingers, she moved the mainspring, shifted the cogs, and pushed the crank back into place. Harriet had watched her father at work for years. She knew the parts and the tools. She knew the methods and the tricks. Harriet had been given simple repairs to complete; she'd even built her own watch, which ticked quietly in her shirt pocket. Harriet's father had never meant for her to follow in his footsteps. But that night, she knew exactly what to do to mend the bearded child.

Once Tilly was patched and cleaned and wound up, Harriet carried her out into the oily dark. Harriet knew if there were clockworks in town, it meant the circus would be camped on the outskirts. She took Tilly back to her home. Harriet stayed too.

Helping the clockworks with their repairs and niggles seemed the most natural thing to do. An over-wound spring, a missing coil, a worn rack hook; Harriet's skills were much needed and welcomed by her new family.

Five years on, and old Alfredo, the ringmaster, had wound down for the last time. Harriet swapped her stolen coat for Alfredo's gold braid jacket. The top hat had stayed. She chose to bind her breasts under the jacket. The circus was already pushing boundaries with a clockwork freak show. They all agreed, a female ringmaster was a step too far.

The marching band struck up in the ring. Loud and slightly off-key. The condensation in the tent played havoc with the tuning.

"You look very pretty, Tilly. Did they wind you up?"

Tilly nodded and waddled off to the wings.

Harriet lifted the base of the tent and whistled to Stan, her deputy. He ran over and crouched down to listen.

"I'll open the show, but I need you to take over."

He crawled under the flap and stood up, dusting off his knees and palms. She ignored his furrowed brow. Stan was a rigger, and he knew trouble as well as he knew a reef knot from a timber hitch.

Harriet's mouth was dry. She could hear the blood rushing through her ears over the sounds of the circus. It dulled the hubbub of the crowd and the squeaks and calls of the animals. She brushed the smut from her white breeches and stretched her neck from side to side. Already old when she'd acquired it from its previous owner, the leather sweatband of her top hat was worn and cracked like her hands. She smoothed the nap. Her forehead was sweaty, and she rubbed it with the back of her hand. As was customary, she placed the hat at a jaunty angle, so it tilted over her right eye.

In the ring, the clowns, with their painted faces, enormous noses, and over-sized shoes, were working the crowd. The audience erupted with shouts and laughter.

The stagehands, either side of Harriet, tugged back the curtains, and she strode into the arena, arms spread wide in welcome.

"Ladies and gentlemen, boys and girls. Welcome to the Freak Show!"

The audience whooped and stamped, and as Harriet lowered her hands, they quietened down. She commanded silence like a priest at a funeral.

The band launched into their fanfare. Up in the flies, Karina and Tomas sparkled. Karina's clockwork wheel gripped the tightrope. In the apex of the tent, it was impossible to see where Karina ended and her unicycle started. A complicated system of cogs drove the wheel round, pumped her tin legs up and down and fired out clouds of smoke which hung in the air like summer clouds. Below the unicycle, attached at the hub, hung the trapeze bar, to which Tomas was fixed by his wind-up 'show' hands. Fully wound, Tomas could make twenty revolutions round the bar: backwards, forwards, and feet-through-first.

All eyes were on the trapeze, so Harriet backed up to the entrance where she could survey the crowd and watch Royston. He stared up at Karina and Tomas. She'd disappear while he was distracted.

Outside the curtain, she handed the jacket to Stan. When he pulled the sleeve over the shiny brass casing of his clockwork shoulder, she heard the catch of the cog she had yet to repair, and she felt a pang of guilt.

"Everything alright?"

"Yes." Harriet didn't trust herself to say more.

She ignored the tight-lipped shake of his head, and after a quick squeeze to his elbow, she ducked under the flaps. The breeze was cool on her sweaty face. Outside in the fading light, she squinted while her eyes adjusted. The horses snorted and tossed their heads, so their feather plumes shook, and the eyes of the peacock feathers sparkled the same blue as Karina's costume.

The elephant, tethered to a lone tree, was silhouetted against the setting sun as if she stood on some distant plain. She trumpeted and pulled against the chain, agitated by the noisy crowds.

Harriet skirted the animal enclosure to get to her tent. She walked past the water trough where the midges dispersed and regrouped like quicksilver.

Inside her tent, she kicked off her boots and grabbed the bag from under the bed. The handles were covered in a thin layer of dust. She bit her lip. Shirt removed; she unwound the bandages that hid her female shape with quick, deft movements. The cloth unravelled with her thoughts. The fabric of the binding grazed the puckered skin on her back. Although she no longer scrutinised her marks in the mirror, it was hard to forget that the shiny, rucked scar tissue spelt 'bitch'.

At the sound of a grunt, Harriet turned round. Royston swayed in front of the tent flap, staring at her breasts.

"There you are, Harriet Harper. I've been looking for you for a very long time, Wife." Her husband stood in the entrance, bleary with alcohol, red-faced and vengeful. His lips were pulled back in a drunken sneer.

She could smell his sour breath. Harriet grabbed the shirt off the bed and covered herself.

"Get out of here." Her reedy voice betrayed her. She was backed into a corner, the side of the tent cold against the flesh of her back.

"You know how this ends," he said, pointing at her bag. "I'm not leaving without you." He lunged at her, and she dodged his grasp but tripped and landed awkwardly on the bed.

She heard the slick of the knife. Royston shoved her down. Before she could recover herself, he'd straddled her, trapping her wrists under his knees. Harriet was strong from rigging and loading, but Royston was a big, heavy man. She kicked her legs. Twisted her hips. The bubble of fear she'd kept locked in her gut for so long rose to the surface and lodged in her gullet.

"Let me go." She tried to keep her voice measured, reaching for the muscles that would lower her tone to her ringmaster level.

Royston threw back his head and laughed. Spittle strands vibrated between his lips like harp strings. His knees ground into her tendons. The buckles on his boots dug into her ribs. She tried to twist out from his grip, and the cool tip of his knife pressed into her throat. She tensed. A hot tear rolled down her face, and she gritted her teeth.

"Time to get reacquainted."

The whimper came, uninvited. She dry-spat at him.

And then the room erupted. Hands grabbed Royston from behind. Over his shoulder, Harriet saw Stan and two riggers. They yanked Royston off her. The knife clanged on the floor. He was dragged out of the tent and into the field.

Harriet wrestled herself into her shirt and rushed after them, grabbing a lamp to find her way in the fading light.

Royston's boots made jagged furrows in the dirt. He bellowed and fought, but they hauled him to the water trough and held his head under until he spluttered and gasped for air. Still struggling, he shouted and swore as they manhandled him past the lions' cage, where the big cats snarled with wrinkled muzzles and yellow fangs; past the restless horses that whinnied and reared; past the corner of the main tent and out towards the tree where the elephant was tethered.

Waves of cheers and laughter escaped from the Big Top. The elephant moaned her annoyance from the field. The ground was warm under foot. Harriet stumbled over rocks and tussocks as she picked up her pace into a run. By the time she reached them, the men had lashed Royston to the elephant's tree.

"Just say the word, Harriet..." The implication was clear.

She looked from Stan to Royston and back. No one would ever know. She could be free. But the years away from Royston had worn the bad memories like pebbles on a beach. She couldn't say the words. Or could she?

Royston roared and strained at the rope. The elephant trumpeted and jerked her chain. Harriet placed the lamp on the uneven ground and wiped the sweat from her face with the edge of her shirt before rubbing her sore wrists.

Unbalanced, the lamp toppled, and the contents and burning wick spilled and trickled onto a patch of tinder-dry grass. Like a mountain stream always finds the sea, the oil found its way to the dead stalks. The patch caught fire with ease. Flames licked the air and snaked across the field.

The elephant spooked, squealed like rusty hinges, and reared up onto her hind legs, pawing at the air. She landed with a thump that made the ground shudder and backed into the tree. Later, Simon the elephant keeper would recall the sickening crunch. While he scrubbed the rust-coloured stain from the elephant's thick hide. Picking pieces of bone from her wrinkled skin, he would play the scene over in his head.

Alarmed by the elephant's squeals, he'd run to her aid. He'd remember the sucking squelch as he led her away from the tree, whispering assurances in her leathery ear and swallowing back saliva from the metallic tang in the air. Only Harriet's sympathetic smile had reassured him the elephant wouldn't be blamed.

Harriet stomped out the fire and joined the men, mesmerised by Royston's broken body. He gurgled and wheezed.

"Let's go." Stan started to walk away.

"Wait."

The men stood panting like impatient dogs.

Harriet straightened her shirt, tucked her hair behind her ears, and chewed on her lip. The men had all half turned to leave.

But Harriet stood firm. It was time to save herself. Arms folded across her chest, she sniffed.

"I can fix him," she said.

"What?" Stan shook his head.

"I can fix him.' She nodded, more for herself than anyone else. "Take him to the workshop."

***

Harriet worked alone for several days and nights. She tinkered, soldered, and tapped. Sometimes, she sent out for a brass wheel blank or a click spring. Sometimes, the crew would hear a whoop or a curse. Sometimes, they thought she must be asleep, for all they heard was the wind as it moaned through the rope holes. But finally, she emerged from the workshop with dark rings under her eyes and grease under her fingernails.

She blinked in the sunlight.

"He needs a glass coffin," she told Stan.

"Is he dead?" Stan didn't hide the hope.

"No. We have a Starving Groom for our Starving Bride, so he'll need a coffin, too." The glazier was summoned, and by the time they'd set up camp in the next town, Royston was placed in his coffin beside his new bride, Lucy. The Starving Bride was the main attraction at the sideshow. In a regular circus, a newlywed would lie in a glass coffin and starve herself, to win a prize of two-hundred and fifty pounds – if she could last for a month.

Lucy was the circus's best kept secret. Customers were happy to see strength and agility enhanced by clockwork, but self-punishment and degradation was human, through and through.

Ladies would peer into the coffin and swoon at Lucy's gaunt face and bony ankles. They were aghast at how she could push herself to such limits for love (and enough money to set her up for life.)

And now, Lucy had a groom. The star-crossed lovers lay side by side, on their Strange Honeymoon, slowly shrinking with 'starvation'. They were watched through clouded glass by gents who sniffed into handkerchiefs and girls who shivered in horrified delight.

Harriet held the curtain back for Tilly to squeeze into the sideshow tent. The child tottered over to Lucy's coffin, pressed her hands and nose up against the cold glass, and waited for Lucy to open her eyes and grin at Tilly. Lucy lay in white lace, looking like a doll in an oversized dress. Over the last few days, her coils had tightened, and the springs had constricted. Her body shrank, and her skin stretched taut over mechanical ribs and protruding hip bones, until she looked Starved for Love.

Harriet lifted the lid off Lucy's coffin and let down the side on its hinges. She handed a small brass key to Tilly. This was Tilly's favourite job in the circus. She lifted Lucy's bodice, and Tilly slotted the key into the brass keyhole in Lucy's side. She turned the key slowly, and it click-clicked round. A money spider tiptoed across the lace of Lucy's cuff and disappeared into the folds of her skirt. When the key resisted, Tilly took it out and handed it back to Harriet. Lucy had grown. Her cheeks were full and round. Her arms filled the sleeves. Her thighs were thick, and her belly was round again. Lucy swung her legs over the side and hopped down from the plinth, then she scooped Tilly up and lifted the child up above her head to squeals of delight.

The women embraced, enveloping the giggling girl between them. Harriet held the flap back, and Lucy ducked out into the night with a smiling Tilly on her hip. At the side of Royston's coffin, Harriet leaned over to look at him through the glass. His face was a death mask, lean and sallow. He looked old and frail, his clothes swamping what was left of his frame.

Harriet huffed at a dirty mark on the glass and rubbed at it with her sleeve. Royston's eyes blinked open, woken by the squeak. She lifted the lid and lowered the side. He reeked of body odour and bad breath and defeat.

She stepped back a pace and fumbled under her collar for the purse she kept around her neck. Nestled inside were two silver keys. One had a corkscrew pin and a long shank; the other had a cruciform pin with a four-way pattern. Both were unique. Neither could be replicated.

Harriet unbuttoned his shirt. Royston groaned, unable to talk. She hadn't replaced his tongue. The keyholes gleamed in the flickering lamp light, still shiny and new. She screwed in the first and then slid in the second. He tried to grab her wrist with his scrawny hand, but the leather restraints jolted him back. She shushed him and bent over as if she meant to kiss his forehead.

"You belong to me now," she whispered and turned the keys.

'All that Glisters'

Orla had known from the beginning that he was a changeling child. She watched over him while he slept, mesmerized by his beauty. When she opened the shutters, the gossamer hair on his skin rippled like corn in the breeze. His skin shimmered, pearlescent in the pale moonlight. The scent was intoxicating; she could nurse him for hours, drinking in his heady aroma. And his eyes changed through a rainbow of colours from one day to the next.

She knew he was a changeling because she loved him more than she'd ever loved any of her other children.

The magic was unexpected. Every night, with the shutters wide open to the moon's glow, she slumbered while holding his tiny fingers. An energy pulsated through her, and the baby spoke in her dreams. "Plant your seeds at the next full moon, for an overnight frost comes unannounced." Or "Mistress Timpkin will pay handsomely to learn she will be with child before first snow." Each morning, Orla woke invigorated, revitalised, regenerated.

She kept baby Jared hidden and secret. She vowed never to give him back. She knew the fairies would come for him when he was grown, but she would be ready to fight for him.

Jared taught her to glister. She used the glister to hide him from the townsfolk and, she hoped, from the fairies. The glister masked his true countenance. Already, he looked old beyond his years, the wrinkles on his brow, the whiskers, the white hairs at his temple.

One night, as she gazed at his perfect nails and smooth, pink palms, he reached into her heart and said, "It's time for me to go to my brethren. This is farewell, my Orla."

Pain ripped through her. "But you are still a baby, Jared," she wailed. She held him tight and begged him to stay.

"The seasons have come and gone. I am grown." The baby slipped from her arms and unfolded until he stood before her in the true visage of the fairy boy turned man. He handed her a looking glass. Through tear-filled eyes, she saw an old woman staring back at her. Fine, grey strands of hair framed a face with a thousand crevices. In the reflection, she looked through to a dark, empty house where cobwebs hung from every corner.

"You tricked me, changeling." She grasped his wrist with a gnarled hand, but he shook her free with little effort.

"Did I, Orla?" Jared's smile was not unkind.

"Please, leave me the glister," she said.

"You have until sunrise," he said.

Jared flickered between Orla's world and his own. He left the old woman admiring herself in the looking glass. She tossed her head and laughed with her glister self; invigorated, revitalised, regenerated.

Thin Places

I wiggle my toes in the pile of used silicone suits at my feet. The jellied mess slaps at my ankles. I'd lift my feet clear but at 620lbs, I can barely lift my eyelids, so...

The sanitiser hasn't cleaned up the old silicone. Or me. In the corner, it should be seated in the charger, but it's tilted at a weird angle. Something covered in fluff has stuck to its pins and stopped it from connecting to the port. On its side, the dying ember of its power light blinks sporadically in the shadows of my room.

And I can't get over to plug it back in.

I could call Dennis.

From the next room come squeaks and huffs and hisses. A rhythmic psst, psst, psst. A whistle of a tyre pump. A wheeze, a whisper, a squeal. Punctuated, of course, by the occasional BANG! Followed by Dennis cursing. Living with a balloon artist is like living next door to a rat festival.

He'll be in when he's finished. The cleaner can wait.

I'm ready to go again. Even though I can feel scraps of old gel behind my ears and between my fingers.

I can reach my SpyneSync, which I grab, plug in, and flick the switch.

It's important to get my posture right before the silicone mould sets to my position. Four hours in 'Thin Places' with tense shoulders when my neck misaligned is uncomfortable and even damaging. I don't want to end up at the Med-bay again for speed-chiro. The chiro bots were brutal.

Eyes closed, I roll my neck, listening for the satisfying click and crunch. I take some deep, calming breaths. The silicone sucks and squelches, tugging the fine hairs on my cheeks until it finds its level.

Some of the reviews of TP 5.7 complained the new silicone was constrictive and felt claustrophobic. But I'm a convert; I like the tight fit – it makes me feel safe. And slim.

That moment when the VR console connects to your neck port is the worst; the click, the crescendo of a whistle, the stomach-dropping surge in your sternum as if you've just jumped off a skyscraper. And the overriding feeling of panic. I adjust the headset and wait for the nanogel to settle around my eyes. My ears pop and bubble as the gel seeps in. It fills every orifice and moulds itself round my shape. This is the bit I like the least.

The command display appears, and I punch the skip command four times. I know the protocol. I understand the risks. I'm impatient to start.

I love the moment the mists clear, and the virtual world becomes reality. I never use the default starting place. I don't want to wake up alone in my virtual 'apartment'. I enter the experience at "The Commute."

Oh, the commute. I want the crush of bodies against me as we squeeze through the tube train doors. I want to shimmy my slender hips between suited men with their musk cologne and minty breath. I want to feel their leg muscles against mine. Our tectonic plates shifting, settling, warm. The feel of my pert breasts pushed up by my own arms as our menage-a-trois squirms and fidgets and sighs.

The train pulls into a station, and there's an orgy of change. Wriggling eels. Some slither onto the platform, while others shoulder their way into the melee. Angles and elbows, the unforgiving edges of bones and buckles, nudge and jar until pieces of body wedge together like an ill-fitting jigsaw puzzle. With a lurch, the train sets off, and there's a suck of separation, then back to noses in other people's hair, and garlic and alcohol sweat from pores.

I slip into a spare seat and smooth my pencil skirt over pencil legs. This virtual body will never bore me. In real life... I don't even want to think about real life.

I'm propped either side by the slumped forms of two men. One has his head back against the train window. The tinny sound of a base beat emanates from his ear buds. A Velcro strap on his cargo pants grazes my leg, as he relaxes his knees. On the other side, an older man, a silver-fox of a man, reads a book on a tablet. His knee rests against mine. I pull my knees together and feel my quads tighten. Oh, to have muscles that respond and move.

My neighbours both man-spread. I shrink. Manspreading. Woman-shrinking. A woman shrinking.

And that is the promise. Thin Places PLC promises to shrink me.

Their advert plays on every media platform, every televised channel, every automated billboard, every skyscraper display. If you don't know about Thin Places, you must be living under a rock. On the moon. Although, I think they just won advertising rights on the mining colonies.

'Shopper's Paradise.' The tinny voice announces my destination. I stand up and hold on to the leather strap, marvelling at the contours of my toned biceps. The tube judders to a halt, and I push through bodies and step into the warm, stale air of the underground.

'Alice!'

My brother's voice hisses loud in my ear. My brain tries to marry the sensation of his breath on my face with the sensation of walking through the echo-filled tunnels that lead to the escalator.

'Alice.'

I land back in the room as if I've been thrown out of an airplane. My head snaps back, and I gasp for air, grasping like a dropped baby.

'You switched me off mid-session. You could have killed me, you twat.' I glare.

***

How do you know if you have a puncture? Well, however hard you try to fill up, you still feel empty. You pump and pump and stuff and cram, but all the glad keeps leaking out. And it might take a while, but one day you think, *Oh. I have a puncture. I'm leaking happy all over the place.*

How to fix a puncture

You will need:

Bubble bath; excellent recall of historical insults, comments and throwaway remarks; credit card; fresh supply of sycophantic associates and so-called friends; fully loaded treats cupboard; charged glass.

1. Find the hole: Immerse punctured object in hot, soapy water. Reminisce about bathtime as a child. How things were so much simpler then. How bodies didn't matter at home – just empty plates. Remember how the other kids whistled the Laurel and Hardy theme tune when you walked to school with your skinny twin. How Dennis reminded you that he was much funnier than Laurel. And he was. He had to be.

2. Mark it: Bubbles will appear where the air leaks out. Mark the hole with a marker, or a kiss, or a pinch. Try not to mistake

the big sighs and the teardrops as the leak. Remember the hole may not be visible to the naked eye. It might feel like it's in your stomach but it's most certainly in your heart.
3. Apply a patch: Roughen up the hole with sandpaper, or some bullying, snide comments, passive aggressive suggestions, even a little emotional blackmail. Stick on a patch – some make-up, a new top, change your hair, try a new diet. There are books and classes and spas and gyms and sex. Any combination of these will serve as a sticking plaster. Or patch.
4. Re-inflate repaired object: Pump up with hot air – You look well. Have you lost weight? You look greeaaat. Fwit fwoo etc, etc. (See also: social media, photoshop, and liturgy of so-called friends.)
5. Repeat: When the hot air starts to wane, replace with doughnuts, crisps and alcohol, until you notice the leak again. Refer to number 1.
<u>Please note:</u> This will not work for balloons. Punctured balloons should be disposed of with care. This will only work for tyres, inner tubes, blow-up beds, or thick-skinned, fat girls – find the leak, patch the hole, refill, and repeat.
Warning: Never patch more than three times.
Three times in a week, a month, a year? Ever?

***

Dennis never knocks; however, he's often preceded by an announcement of his latest creation, and a short speech or a display of (in)appropriate animal or mechanical noises. This short interlude should, in theory, give me time to cover my modesty or wake up. It never does.

'Condom Narwhal!'

Said narwhal with its overly long tusk, ribbed for extra sensation, ruts the door frame, accompanied by Dennis' sound effects, 'Eurgh, eurgh, eurgh.'

'Hen party,' Dennis explains and swims the creature into my room. 'Condoms are surprisingly fragile.' He roots in his pocket and brings out a handful of split and exploded rubbers, a rainbow of slime covered mess, a graveyard of disintegrated plastic shreds. With a grin, he stuffs it all back in his pocket and wipes his hand down his trousers. He sniffs his hand and grimaces. 'I smell like a knocking shop.'

Dennis looks round the room, and his gaze rests on me. 'Hungry? You want me to make a sandwich or something?'

If I close my eyes, it could be our mother in the room. His voice has the same tone, the same cadence. Of course, she wouldn't have asked. She'd have barged in with a plate of sandwiches and crisps on a tray with a napkin and a small dish of grapes or apple (because that's healthy).

'No thanks. I'm just about to sync up,' I say and nod at the three-quarter-full bag suspended from the drip stand. 'Lunch is covered.'

He screws up his nose. 'Okay. I've got a dozen cock and balls to make for bunting.'

'Am I...do I look any different?' I hate the whine I can hear in my voice and regret the question immediately. Dennis would never say anything to upset me, and he hates lying.

'You are my beautiful sister. I don't know why...you are lovely the way you are.'

I feel my lips twitch down in disappointment, and he adds, 'but I think maybe your jawline is a bit sharper?'

I muster a smile. 'It always goes off my face first. So that's good, isn't it?'

'Keep up the good work, sis. Better get on. Laters.'

Before the door closes behind him, the horny narwhal assaults the doorknob and swims off with snorting giggles. I'm about to call after Dennis when he shouts, 'I know,' and slams the door shut.

***

I can't remember the last time I left the chair. I've finished my session in Thin Places. Well, it un-synced me under their safety feature. It doesn't feel like I spent fourteen hours there. The drip-feed pack is almost empty. I reach down my left thigh and tug on the waste bag – it's full. Maybe it was fourteen hours, then.

I summon the sanitiser. It whirs and skids over the varnished floorboards to my feet. While the main portal sucks at the silicone gel on the floor, spindle arms ratchet out and disconnect the waste bag from my catheter, replacing it with a fresh one with magician moves. I half expect it to say, 'Ta-da!' Those same spindle arms unhook the feed bag and hang up a full one from the store in the machine's side panel. The stamp on the bag reads 'Day 677.'

Outside the window, the sun is setting in a radiant sky. Feathered clouds weave across the different shades of pink and orange. A short walk away is the city park, which at this time of year will be a riot of verdant green. A short excruciating walk lined with staring faces and judgemental noises. It's fine, there's a beautiful park in Thin Places where I can picnic and swim in the lake.

It's fine.

Once the sanitiser has seated itself on the charger plate, the room is hushed and still. Dust motes dance in the shards of light through the net patterns.

Next door, Dennis huffs and puffs his infinite Big Bad Wolf efforts. I listen to the melody of his breaths. Long, strong gasps when he's blowing up the elongated twisting balloons; shorter, quick breaths for legs and ears. Often, I can tell by the squeak and silence pattern, which object he's practicing: swords, crowns, poodles – a lot of squeaking and Dennis yapping.

Today, he tells me, he is working on a special project; something so big, he'll need to pre-expand parts of it here at home and transport them to the venue for construction. He wants to bring the sections in for me to guess what he's making. I'm preparing myself for a parade of body parts or confusing balloon mechanics.

There's a familiar crack followed by, 'Oh bollocks.' The pump has broken. I wait for the slam of his door, tumbled footsteps down the stairs and the bustle and crash of him in his stock room.

Instead, there's the long slow tpffff of Dennis blowing up a balloon himself. There is a pause as he inhales with the lung capacity of a free diver.

I hear a weird snap and hiccough, followed by a rasping sound. And then a piece of furniture clatters to the floor.

A cold panic envelops me from my head down.

'Dennis?' I call out.

It sounds like a sock being sucked up by a hoover which becomes a strangled, choked wheeze.

Something hard and heavy bashes against our joining wall. *Oh God.*

I must move. *Can I move?* It's been so long. *Get a grip.*

I pull out the IV drip wedged into the retention disk by my belly button. The green bag of gloop that's feeding me nutrients and helping me shed weight (supposedly), splatters to the floor and oozes liquid into a grey puddle (not actually green, then?) My catheter and bag will have to come with me.

I roll myself back to build up momentum, but I can only move my head. I place my hands on the arms of the chair and brace myself. With my feet tucked back, the chair apron presses against my calves.

Next door, table legs scrape, and the rasping has changed to a croaked hiss.

I press down into the armchair and watch the flesh on my arms shake with the effort. I have the bingo wings of a 747, great pillows of fat that tremble as I try to push myself to stand.

My stomach is so big now I can't tell it apart from my thighs. Mountains of fat-filled skin slide down to my knees as I push to stand upright. I walk round the armchair like a giant toddler, thighs chafing, the bulk of me swaying, a huge fleshy pendulum. Holding on to furniture and sweating, I shuffle to the door. My vision starts to tunnel, but I take deep breaths. The door won't open far; and I block it with my expanse. I manage to squeeze through.

Maybe I have lost some weight?

The hallway smells stale and musty like my nan's old house. The striped flock wallpaper is caked with dust and cobwebs. The banister is sticky. I pull myself along the hallway, uneasy step by uneasy step. Dennis's door swings back, and his brass handle smashes into a ready-made indentation.

Dennis is bent over, retching. Where the strength comes from, I don't know, but I'm behind him. I thump him hard on the back.

Thwack! He flies into the table and staggers. I drop to my knees, and land on the flesh of my stomach. Excruciating. This pitches my body forward, and I can't stop the slam into Dennis, who's flattened to the floor. He spits out a red balloon. Slimy and shiny, it slides to the carpet, while he sucks in air and splutters and coughs under me. He's shaking.

'Get off me!' His voice breaks.

And I realise he is laughing. Uncontrollably. He turns his face to me. Tears are streaming down his cheeks, leaving smudged rivulets. He chortles like a cartoon dog, 'Shee, shee, shee, shee, shee!'

And we're nine again, sitting cross-legged on the floor in front of the lectern in the big hall at school. Mr Day has clasped his hands on the top of the stand to lead us in morning prayers.

Dennis whispers in my ear, 'Sausages.'

And our bodies convulse and shake and grunt with the force of strained laughter that builds like a pressure cooker. Tears fill our eyes, and we purse our lips, trying to cork the noise. I can still feel the bone of his shoulder juddering against mine, and our knees knocking together with suppressed hysteria.

We're helpless with giggles, lolling on the floor, just like when we were kids.

'I can't get up. Can you shove me? Or sort of pull me up?'

In the end, I manage to half roll, half slide off and raise myself up on one elbow. 'Are you okay? Can you breathe now?'

Dennis nods and wipes the drool from his chin and pockets the red balloon husk.

From my vantage point on the floor, I look round his room. 'I'd forgotten your *planets and astronauts* wallpaper,' I say and notice that he has a double bed now and a different duvet cover in bachelor black.

Through tear-filled eyes, Dennis says, 'I've missed you, Alice.'

I grin. 'Well, there's another fine mess you've gotten me in to.'

Dennis whistles the Laurel and Hardy tune until he erupts into a coughing fit.

'I've missed you, too.'

Dennis straightens the table and rights the chair. He clears his throat again – it must be sore. I'm still on the floor, trying to work out how to get back on my feet.

I crawl to his bed, and with a lot of heaving and heavy breathing, I manage to pull myself up to sitting position.

'I think I may have had enough of Thin Places,' I say. 'I want to see downstairs again.'

Dennis, still coughing, has pulled a red canister out from his built-in wardrobe. To my confusion, he pops the short tube in his mouth, turns the valve, and sucks in an enormous mouthful. He turns to me and in a high-pitched, helium-fuelled voice squeaks, 'Could you help me build a condom unicorn first?'

Made of Straw

Tallulah was made of straw. A dried-out husk of a woman. Often trampled, chewed, stuffed, broken, and quick to ignite.

She shoved the brittle ends of her hair into her hat and wrapped the scarf round her neck. At the front door, she glanced sideways into the hall mirror. I belong in a field, she thought, with birds pecking at my ears and the wind whistling through my emptiness. Only the cat heard her hollow laugh.

Outside, the gusts rattled the gate with impatience. Alright, I'm coming, she thought, some of me, at least. Leaning into the north-easterly, she trudged down the lane. Buffeted and blown, as she had in all her life, she went where the wind blew her. Past the church, where the crows perched on headstones wiping their beaks and fixing her with dead black eyes.

Across the village green, where she twisted her ankle in rabbit holes. Along the hedgerows by Crampton's farm. The cows lumbered to the hedge to watch her trip down the lane. She was like their cud, regurgitated to be chewed on again.

A robin broke off its song and flew across her path. Tallulah wasn't alone. Someone was sitting at the bus stop. Except it hadn't been a bus stop for many years, just a dilapidated shack with two remaining sides and a slatted roof. A tune was being whistled, and a foot was wagging. It wore a brown brogue and bright red sock. Or socks. Presumably, there was another foot with a matching sock and shoe, attached to another leg, attached to a man. The wind nudged her to the shelter. She peeped in at the occupant.

"No buses stop here," she said.

"That's okay. I'm not waiting for a bus." He smiled. His eyes were cornflower blue.

Tallulah's mouth was dry as a wheat husk, but something stirred in the hole in her chest.

"What are you waiting for?" she asked. The sun peeped out from behind the ochre clouds, and he shielded his eyes to look at her.

"I'm waiting for you."

The wind had dropped. He glowed in the sunlight, and Tallulah could feel the weight of her limbs. Her stomach muscles clenched. She could hear a steady beat in her ears. A pulse. Her heart. And his tapping foot moved in time with it.

"Why are you waiting for me?"

"I'm waiting for you to dance, Tallulah," he said and started to whistle his tune again.

The music stirred in her neck, grasped her round the waist and spun her into the lane. She stretched out her arms and turned round and around. She kicked out her legs and jigged and skipped. Muscles groaned, but Tallulah danced. And she laughed. She laughed like a peel of bells on a summer's eve.

Then she was dancing with the man, holding his hot hand, resting her other hand on his shoulder, feeling his bones through the soft fabric of his jacket. They twirled and twisted; they spiralled and swivelled.

She pulled off her hat, and her yellow hair sprang into glossy curls. She tugged off her scarf, and the colour rose to her cheeks, making her face shine.

"I never heard this music before," she said.

"You never listened before," he said, "That's why I've been waiting."

Tallulah let the music fill her emptiness. And the man led her down the lane. The music came from all around now, in the bushes, on the breeze, out of the fields and up in the trees. Arm in arm, the two of them ran down the lane. Tallulah's cheeks ached from smiling, and her feet throbbed. But it felt good and solid and real.

The man was an alchemist.

Tallulah was made of gold.

Hunt

Snow clouds hang heavy and low, sagging under their burden, filling the sky with an ochre light. A branch snaps, and a layer of snow slides to the ground.

Sasha stops. And waits. Her ears strain for the crunch of steps or a snort or a snuffle. He's there, somewhere through the trees. His lumbering steps leave divots the size of dinner plates. She sees him now and stretches herself tall and thin and invisible behind a pine.

Above her, a bird flutters and dusts her with icing-white flakes. She's cross-eyed from watching one melt on her nose.

His grunts echo through the still woods. She freezes, holding her hand over her mouth to stifle the cry that wants to shatter the silence and avalanche her grief. Her head fills with thoughts of sticky brown fur and the bellow, and the slash of rapier claws. And her father gurgling, 'Run, Sasha, run!' How he'd goaded the bear by crawling into the forest, and how the last thing she saw of him were his boots, kicking and shaking their macabre dance.

She couldn't outrun the beast, who was fuelled by anger and hungry for her blood. She couldn't hide from his raised head that sniffed the air and followed her trail.

He's close now. He stinks of rotting flesh and honey, sickly sweet. The smell of death. Hot breath plumes from his muzzle, still stained pink. She wonders if the matted hairs are wet with her father's blood.

Sasha backs round the gnarled trunk, her gloves catching on splinters, and peeps out behind him. His huge hind quarters roll and dip, little balls of snow dangling from the fur on his paws. His muscles move under the pelt, shoulders undulating, powerful and sure.

A low growl resonates through his body, making the fur quiver in an earthquake of ripples. He turns his heavy head and stares. Red drool drips in globules and lands in the snow as he swings his body round to face her.

She stands straight and still.

The bear leans back and unfolds until he's several feet taller than her. He roars, rotating his muscle-bound neck so the sound fills every corner of the canopy. His foetid breath blows the hair from her face, and his spittle sticks to her cheeks.

She throws her head back and roars, too. Roars for her father, roars for herself, and roars herself ready to do what she should have done before.

The startled bear wavers.

She cocks the gun, brings it up to her shoulder, squints through the sights, and her finger brushes the cold metal of the trigger.

She can hear her father saying, 'Feet apart, one just in front of the other. Butt to your shoulder. Finger on the trigger. Get it in your sights. Take your time. Then breathe, Sasha. Remember to breathe.'

She pulls the trigger and shoots, her shoulder absorbing the punch. The bear jolts backwards with a squealing whimper, and slumps to the ground. A red stain melts the snow under its slack jaw.

'That's for my dad,' she says. But the pain in her heart is still there. How will she remember to breathe without him?

Inside Out

She wears her coat inside out, because this is the only way she can breathe. The loose threads and frayed hems float, absorbing the sticky air. She prefers the smooth flat edges of the seams against her skin, although the worn pile of the fabric catches on the rough flakes of her elbows, and sticks like limpets to her fossilized bones.

She drifts as if she were seaweed, pushed and pulled through the murky streets of the city. People pass like fish: glassy eyed and open-mouthed, staring down at their bright rectangular lures. They bump and jostle, caught in a net, swimming in different directions, oblivious to their fate.

She swims against the crowd, diving deeper into the abyss.

At the city limits, houses shimmer either side of the narrow streets, like slimy walls of underwater caves. They loom over her, blocking out the light. She's a diver exploring corroded passageways and inky blue depths. When she stops to look at an oily puddle that's oozed onto the path, the reflection of the stars makes her stomach flip as if she stares into the Mariana Trench. She steadies herself, her nails clutching at crumbled coral walls.

Sometimes, all that's left is the past. It opens its yawning maw, and she floats in, a small piece of spectral, and rudderless, plankton. Family, friends, house, all gone, washed away with the tides of misfortune.

A pub door opens, and sounds and smells spill onto the pavement, along with raucous laughter and the yeasty smell of stale beer. She feels her way along the bricks and holds the doorframe, trying to pull herself out of the depths and into the light.

"Easy, darling." A bulk blocks her way, broad-shouldered, dead eyed. He circles her, nudges her, sniffs the air. "You don't want to go in there, love, it's about to get messy." He smiles, and his teeth glint in the pub's neon sign.

She's being steered away from the shallows. Bumped and bustled through the door into the cavernous depths.

"I'll come with you. You can't even dress yourself. Let's get that coat off, shall we?" And it sounds kind and cold and calculated.

But she shrugs off the inside-out coat as her eyes scan the shoal of spirits that seem to dart about behind the bar. She realises, too late, she is caught.

Sister

It has become an obsession.

Lilith's hand combs through her hair, pulling strands out, shedding them through her own winter. An empty follicle for each empty thought. Each one beats like a clock in her head: tick, tick, tick.

She lies back on the bed and feels under the pillow for her anchor. The anchor is made of the hairs she's collected and formed into a thick sheaf, tied with a black ribbon. Bits of her she leaves behind, so she can come back. *Somewhere, there's baby hair, safe in a box. She can smell the waxy cradle cap and feel how the soft wisps brushed her lips. Is it at her parents' place? Except it doesn't belong to both her parents anymore, only her father.* She tugs at another strand on her head. Never enough to calm the thoughts.

Lilith runs her fingers between the cool cotton sheet and pillowcase, and over the frizzy clump. She feels the comforting tingle on her scalp. She's connected. Her anchor is in place. She can come back. Anytime. Sometime.

She closes her eyes, *five, four, three, two, one,* and she is there. Somnia. The dream world.

The walls of her bedroom glimmer with not-quite-there ripples. She walks across the translucent carpet. It's like swimming over a shelf in Mediterranean waters; pale turquoise gives way to an inky blue abyss. Her stomach lurches, but with the ease of a practised flyer, she launches herself from the diaphanous edge of the nearly-building, out into the air.

And up.

She pushes herself over the flickering rooftops, past the treetops and up, up into the lilac sky of Somnia. The wind whistles past her ears. Trouser legs flap against her skin with the 'fluck fluck fluck,' sound of pigeon wings. The air cools, and she levels out to gaze down on the patchwork fields of rapeseed yellows and new maize greens. She dives through fluffy clouds, lost in the eerie silence of the opaque mists, until she emerges back into the pale sky with a sheen of moisture on her face and hands. She heads for the sea where she can breathe. And be free.

Lilith's breath catches at the thrill of flight. She scans the scene below her as she skims over transparent rooftops and gardens. The occasional movement is an animal scampering into a hedgerow, or a flare of a bush ablaze with autumn colours.

On the horizon, a black ribbon road marks the border to the beach, and in front of her stretches the calm sea. A light breeze ushes gentle waves that make tentative baby steps onto the shore. A flash of auburn glints between the bog oaks, a gleam of bronze in the salt-frosted leaves.

'Mum?' The word bursts from her, a whisper in the dark, a whimper for help from the monsters under the bed. She wonders what the word might have sounded like on a child's lips, how it would have felt in her ears? She can't see what had made her look. It was a trick of the light.

Flying low over the sea, her shadow a leviathan in the deeps, Lilith's salty tears merge with saltier spray. The wind whistles her mother's voice telling her, 'You're so special, my child. One day you'll understand a mother's love...'

One day she had. Not just one. For 549 days, she knew what it was to be a mother. Long enough to understand. But not long enough. She digs her knuckles into her eye sockets and wipes away the tears. With new resolve, she banks right and pushes up and out towards the Borderlands. She hasn't been there for a while. It's time to try again.

The Borderlands' stony shore is unforgiving and treacherous, scattered with huge granite boulders and hemmed with crumbling cliffs. The sea caves form and collapse with surprising regularity like pock sores on the diseased face of the chalk. The coast changes, sometimes dramatically, between visits.

Smells of warm seaweed, fish, and rotten foliage remind her of summer holidays. Hazy days on cool beaches, the sounds smothered by rolling fog. Lilith's mother and aunts would organise treasure hunts for the children. The rules were as loose and shifting as the Borderlands cliffs, but she and her cousins clambered over rocks and slid on seaweed-slick granite. That familiar ache of frustration gnaws at her as she searches now. She jerks at every glint or shimmer, every rustle or crunch. The caves' dead eyes are unyielding as she hugs the shore looking for something. Someone. A sign. Overhead, the gulls' bleating mews like the cries of a baby.

'Lil?' Her shoulder jolts. Her name sounds far away, a whisper. 'Lil,' it nags. Her body tips, and for a moment, she looks back out across the water along the golden path that leads to the sun. Jonathan is trying to wake her. How is it morning already? There's never enough time.

She sighs. At the base of her neck the tiny hairs prickle. Midair, she starts to turn over and prepares for the fade back to reality, when she sees a movement on the top of the cliffs. A lone figure. The woman teeters at the cliff's edge, arms spread wide, her long flowing robe whipped by the wind. But it's her hair that makes Lilith start; a sunburst of auburn, chestnut, and gold; a halo of rich pulsating colours. The figure disperses into a million tiny pieces, a swarm of mosquito specks that shift and shape, ball and elongate and then dissipate and disappear.

Lilith surrenders to the shudder of waking up.

When she opens her eyes, the room is bathed in the soft glow of the bedside lamp and Jonathan is looking down at her, eyebrows raised.

'Morning.'

She heaves herself up and leans against the headboard. The fresh mint of his toothpaste hangs in the air like the swarm of specks on the cliff. Her fingers are already rooting in her scalp, pulling out the fine threads one at a time. The sound of the hairs snapping free reverberates through her skull like a gunshot.

'What time is it?'

'Ten past five. You asked me to wake you before I left.'

She hides the collection of hairs under the pillow.

'I was in Somnia.'

'Of course you were.' He moves to the mirror in the wardrobe door and adjusts his tie.

'There was a woman I've never seen before. She had the most amazing hair.'

He stills. 'In your dream?'

'No. I was in Somnia.'

'Yuh huh?'

He's checking his phone with swipes and taps and a half smile.

'I wish you could see what I see.'

'Hmmm?'

'I wish you could see how beautiful and serene it is there.'

'Uh huh.'

'Then you'd understand.'

He smooths his eyebrows in the mirror. His gaze moves to the shelf on his left. She watches as he places the tiny picture frame upright. Every day, she lays it face down. Every day, he stands it back up.

They both stare at the grainy picture. Swaddled in blue, bird-feather eyelashes rest on alabaster cheeks, wet filigree curls frame the screwed-up face. Jonathan's jaw clenches, and his fingers linger on the frame. Lilith shuts her eyes.

'Remember to take your meds.' She recognises the change in his tone. 'Erm, my phone will have to stay on silent. Conferences both days. And I'm back tomorrow night. Don't wait up. I'll be late.'

There was something familiar about the shape of the woman, how she had held her arms and stretched her neck...

'Lil. Lilith. Jeez. I'll see you tomorrow.' He moves her hand from her head, and the copper weaves wrapped around her fingers catch the light of the lamp. She holds them on top of the duvet. Jonathan kisses the top of her head. He pulls the bedroom door closed behind him, harder than needed. She unravels the strands and places them in her bedside drawer with the others.

***

Lilith lies back down, slides her hand between the pillow and the warmth of the sheet and touches the hair. She counts her breaths and pictures the dirty-white cliff faces, the sad-eyed caves.

And she is there, standing on the beach, surrounded by a thick mist. As she takes tentative steps across the pebbles, the granite monoliths slip through the haze to appear suddenly in front of her. She feels her way round them, their rough surfaces icy on her palms. She listens for the hiss of the waves, always to her right. With each step, she tests for solid ground by tapping her toe. The movement reminds her of a ballet dance she did as a child, in a cold hall with an out-of-tune piano and the staccato instructions of the teacher. She remembers goosebumps on her arms; arms that refused to coordinate with her pink nylon legs.

Now, those arms shoot out ahead to save herself when she stumbles. A gasp-giggle explodes from her at the surge of adrenaline, though the sound is swallowed into the dense drizzle that hangs in the air. Her nerves tingle, and her head thumps, and she barely recognises her own hands, disembodied and suspended in the fog.

Out of the smoky swirls, a gaping sea cave opens its mouth, surprised. She launches upwards and follows the cliff face, up to its summit. When she alights on the meadow near the edge, the mist covers the ground in writhing spirals, winding round her ankles, a spectre serpent. The seething layer slithers over the edge of the cliff, merging with the clouds, and the sea is hidden under the vaporous film. All around her is pale and silent.

A figure emerges out of the mist. The woman stops just ahead of Lilith, her robe billowing in a not-there wind. Through the green gauze garment, Lilith can make out the woman's shape; her waist, her hips, her breasts. Up close, she is nothing like Lilith's mother. Her face is slimmer, sharp, angular. And she has so much hair. It drifts out from her head in long colourful fibres spun with gold.

The woman drinks her in with copper-flecked eyes, and her gaze trickles its syrupy caress over Lilith's limbs. Lilith trembles. The woman reaches out for her and runs slender fingers through her hair. Lilith cringes: she hasn't washed it in days, but the woman sighs, and Lilith relaxes.

Taking hold of Lilith's hands, the woman smiles as she speaks. Her lips don't move but the words slosh and suck, they seep into Lilith's head like rock pools filling with sea.

The honey-drizzled voice melts down her hot spine.

Sister. Call me Sister.

It's not her mother. But the cork of disappointment wedged in her throat is dislodged by a bubble of something rising from her sternum that she hasn't felt for a long time.

You're searching for someone. But you've wasted so much time. You want more. I can give you time. Time in exchange for a little of your hair.

On her head, Lilith feels the cold patches, and her fingers graze the baby hairs. *Baby hair.* She wraps her fingers round and pulls a few lengths from her head. The pain is sharp, and the tug makes a cracking sound like a flower being picked. She holds the hairs out to Sister.

'How much?'

Sister's mouth twitches. She doesn't move. Her rainbow mane glistens and quivers, and the filaments of it snake towards Lilith. The blind ends feel for the hairs she offers until the tips join, and Sister's mane assimilates her own.

Like Rapunzel, she feeds the shafts to Sister's hair, length after length, then clumps, some with snowflakes of skin attached. Her scalp stings, but Sister's eyes are closed, and the undulating tresses worm towards her, hungry. Now Lilith uses both hands; snap, snap, snap; in a frenzy of stripping and ripping. Some of it falls to the ground.

Don't waste time. The tentacles of hair reach down, groping, enveloping every fallen fibre.

Lilith's eyes water, but she rakes and grabs handfuls. She feeds the nosing threads of Sister's hair, giving bits of herself away.

'Have it. Take every last piece of it, of me. Only, let me stay.'

Sister lets out an ecstatic gasp as her hair flops to her shoulders, and Lilith staggers back as if released from a spell.

Stay – as long as you need.

They drift apart. Lilith sways, dazed. Sister levitates up out of the mist, rising into the sky. She burns bright like the sun, then explodes into a million stars, and is gone.

'How will I find you?'

You'll find me.

***

Lilith lingers in Somnia as the balance shifts. She wakes only to pick hairs from the carpet, from the sink, from the jackets in the wardrobe, collecting payment for Sister.

Days fossilise. Time becomes arrhythmic and brittle. The structure of the bedroom crumbles like sea caves. The only constant is Somnia. And Sister.

Lilith stays in her bed. Jonathan stops trying to disguise his disgust.

'All you do is sleep.'

He stops leaving tea on the bedside table. He stops kissing her head. He stops slamming the door. He stops coming home.

***

I'm sandwiched between the counsellor's chino trousers and the wrist bone of his left hand. His pen is poised over my fresh, empty page. He's left-handed – an ironic attribute in a counsellor because his words are covered by his arm as he writes and not revealed. Revelation being at the heart of his practice. With his legs crossed, he taps the dangling foot. He stops himself, consciously, because it might convey his impatience and boredom.

My yellow, ruled sheets across his dark brown chinos remind him of sweets from his childhood; chocolate covered bananas, that he and his little brother bought from the corner shop. He remembers the delight in their independence when they were sent off with a pound each to spend. The counsellor squares off a section in the bottom right-hand corner of my page and scribbles shorthand for, *'Journal - childhood memories, choc bananas, thought of Billy today.'* He hasn't written about Billy since sheet twenty-four. In tiny letters, he writes, *Block out calendar for a supervisory.* He encloses the note in a rectangular box – four scored lines. The pen leaves my page for a second before he starts in again with spirals, round and round, covering the words, blocking them in. Or out.

Opposite him, in a matching Ikea Poäng chair, his client sits and sniffs, inspecting his cuticles. Poäng translates as 'punchline' in Swedish. More irony, the punchlines are lame in this room. You have, 'See you next time,' which doesn't have that end-of-a-great-story ping to it. Or there's 'In the best possible way, I hope we don't meet again, but you know where I am should you feel the need...'

The client is a younger man. He wears tight jeans, and his knees jiggle, making the chair quake.

'I don't know why I'm here,' he says without looking up.

'In the questionnaire you talked about feelings of guilt...'

'I wonder if I'd got there sooner, things might have turned out differently?'

The counsellor pauses his pen. 'You were on a break from each other?'

The younger man nods. His forehead furrows into two deep grooves over the bridge of his nose.

The counsellor says nothing. He does this a lot. I reckon he spends three quarters of these sessions saying nothing. He doodles. Leaving space for thoughts. The clock over the door slow ticks through the silence. The counsellor writes the young man's name and the date in the space at the top of my page. On the first line he writes GUILT in capital letters and underscores it twice.

A fat tear runs down the client's face, catching round the bulge of his nose and spilling over his lip. He wipes his nose and mouth with the back of his hand and mumbles, 'Sorry.'

'This is your space. You are safe here. Safe to express yourself. Safe to explore your feelings and emotions. There's no judgement.' The counsellor picks up a box of tissues from the low table between their chairs and offers it to the man.

The man takes the box, removes a tissue, and rests the box on his knees while he blows his nose.

He's taken the box. The whole box. Does the counsellor understand the significance of this? He must. Our client is preparing to cry it all out. He's going to empty himself into those white squares of inadequate paper. He's going to fill the bin with mucus and salty water and regret.

The counsellor has doodled a teardrop under 'guilt.' Inside the teardrop he draws a small curved-edge window shape, a technique to make it look like a reflection, a trick of the light. He raises his knee so I'm angled towards him and out of sight of the client. Engrossed in his sketch, cross-hatching, and shading, he only registers snippets of the client's outpouring,

'...my decision, I'd done all I could...mental health...she wouldn't get help...thought I could use it as leverage...I feel so bad...what if...'

The counsellor has been concentrating so hard on the doodles that he's bent up my left lower corner and ruckled it in three places. He smooths my creases and uses the motion to disguise a glance at his watch. The watch is multi-purpose. It vibrates against my sheets and his wrist to remind him he hasn't completed his quota of steps yet. He flicks his wrist and the display changes to a heart-shaped icon which pulsates in time with his beating heart. The movement interrupts the client who looks up. The counsellor nods and scribbles more notes on me. Again, in shorthand he writes, *so fucking bored.*

With a velvet voice, he draws the session to a close. 'You might try writing it all down in a letter. Write her a letter. Write all the things you wish you'd said. Write out your anger. Write out your sadness. Then just hide the letter away. It can be a cathartic process.' The client's look is blank. 'Helpful,' he adds, helpfully. 'Try it. We can talk about it next time.'

He slides me face down onto the low table and places his pen across my page. After taking back the empty box of tissues and shaking the client's hand, he follows him to the door and sees him out.

He puts the pen in his breast pocket and then rips off my top page before scrunching it into a tight ball and, in a well-practiced move, bounces it off his bicep and into the wastepaper basket.

His watch buzzes again.

This time it reminds him to drink more water. He drains the glass and places it on me, left centre of my clean page. A drip of water slides down the side of the glass and seeps into me, joining the ring of condensation that's already branded through several of my sheets. When he comes to scribble on me later, he will tut at the ruined pages, rip them off and ram then into the bin. He's all about clean starts, he'll joke with the next client.

***

Jonathan shakes Lilith awake. She blinks at him through sleep-crusted eyes.

'I've been trying to wake you for ages. Jeez, you sleep like the dead. What's happened to the rest of your hair? What the fuck have you done to yourself? You look...ill.'

Lilith knows he's more careful with his words when he is being paid by the hour.

'I've used it all up.'

'What?'

'I gave it to Sister. For more time.'

'You're not making any sense, Lilith. It's a mess. You're a mess.'

Jonathan shakes his head and turns to the mirror to inspect his chin.

'I don't know what you think you're doing—' he examines his nostrils, '—but you need to get help. I'll speak to Dr Browning at the clinic. Get her to call you or something. And put on your hat, would you?'

Lilith crawls back under the duvet, and Jonathan rubs his temple, speaking to his reflection.

'I don't have time for this, I'm late. I only came to pick up my stuff. We'll have to talk later.' His voice trails off like his intentions. He scoops up a yellow, ruled legal pad and slides it into his laptop bag. He checks he has his pen in his breast pocket.

A tissue falls to the floor, which he grabs, scrunches into a ball, and bounces off his forearm into the bin.

From the bedroom door, he says what will be his last words to her. 'At least have a shower and get dressed. Just sort yourself out, will you?' And he is gone.

Lilith takes out the last of the hair from under her pillow. Clutching the matted nest to her chest, she stares at the ceiling, deep in thought. In the corner of the room, near a crack, a gossamer spider sits on thread-thin legs, waiting. Lilith feels her own scalp, the smooth patches, and the scabs. She traces the insurmountable lumps and mounds of her skull. Tiny hairs, too short to pull, bristle under her fingers.

With a sigh, she slides into Somnia, like she's slipping into a hot bath.

When she opens her eyes in the Borderlands, everything is different. The colours sing. As she stands on the cliffs, the earth vibrates beneath her feet, and humming grasses brush against her legs. Bright and blue and cloudless, the endless sky stretches above her, and the air buzzes with life. Lilith buzzes too – it makes her skin tingle and raises goosebumps along her arms. Sister is waiting for her. Lilith shows her the bird nest tangles. 'It's all I have left.'

Sister's lip curls, and Lilith's mouth goes dry, but Sister's lips rise into a smile again, and Lilith's heart jumps with anticipation.

Will you stay?

'Yes. I'm staying.'

Sister's hair judders to life. It stretches out, writhing and wriggling towards her, coiling round the knotted mass that Lilith holds out like a gift. It twists and turns, wrapping itself around her wrists and elbows, her ankles and knees, until Lilith is lost in the teeming mass of reds and browns and gold. Past, present, and future melt like soap suds, and Lilith's knees buckle, but the hair tightens and stops her fall.

The persistent ring of a two-tone bell clangs in the distance. She tries to ignore it, but her eyes are prised open. 'I want to stay,' she calls out, but she can't hear Sister over the noise. Nor can she see her through the thick weft of hair. Lilith rolls and rotates in her bindings like a silk dancer.

At her peripheral vision, over the cliff, lights flash as the sun sparkles on the cresting waves. Her name is being called. *Lilith, can you hear me?*

Sister appears in front of her and draws her into an embrace. Lilith succumbs and breathes in a faint scent of vanilla and patchouli. *Mum?*

Clear! Lilith's body jolts, but Sister holds her tighter, and they levitate above the heaving ground. Distanced from the earth, Lilith tears herself from the other world, breaks away from the noise and the thumping sensation in her chest. They rise higher and higher, entwined. There's no tingle at the back of Lilith's neck now, and the lack of connection intoxicates her, elevates her. Through the silence she hears a baby's laugh, gurgling and throaty. The light fades to midnight blue. The sounds diminish to a high-pitched whistle.

And with one final snap, she breaks free.

Heart of Glass

People assumed that because Crystal was made of glass, she was fragile. Brittle. She tried to ignore the looks and stares, the gasps. The kid-glove treatment got on her nerves, the too-gentle touch, the cries of, 'Oh, I'm scared I'll break you.' She learned to live with it: her transparent limbs, her fractal joints, her many-faceted features.

She quite liked the prism she created in the bright morning sky. She quite liked the warm glow she reflected, of the setting sun. She even liked the way raindrops trickled down the perfect symmetry of her long, straight lines.

But she did not like her heart. It didn't work. For all its squishing and pumping, it was no good. It sat under the glacial shelf of her chest, red and membranous and wet. Pressed against the immaculate architecture of her latticed ribs, it pulsated and squelched. It heaved and twitched, leaving an imprint of filigree veins on the faces of her pristine structure. It was ugly. It was messy. And it was broken.

People assumed that because Crystal was made of glass, she was fragile. But the only part of her that had ever been hurt, was made of flesh. She wished she had been born with a heart of glass.

Smoke

Smoke and flames billow into the night sky, blocking out the scudding clouds. The fire rages. The rafters crackle and spit. My face burns in the heat as sweat tickles my temples and groups on my top lip.

I stare at the door, watching the paint shrivel and shrink. The key sits where I left it in the lock, and it glows orange. It looks ready to melt. There would be no getting in, then. Or out.

I picture her inside the scout hut, collapsed on the floor, a charred rigid hand reaching for the exit. Her hair is sizzling, soldered to her scalp. Man-made fibres meld with her skin. Her tendons frazzle, forcing her knees up to her chest. Fingers curl. Spine curves into a charred, foetal, burnt offering.

I've waited so long for this. It's no more than she deserves.

The rest of the group stand behind me, shielding their faces from the heat.

Yes, I'm back at group again. Sometimes I hate them all. I despise their weakness. Their addiction. Their pathetic attempts at justification to keep on doing the thing. And then one of them will manage to quit. Like fully quit and make it right through to the end of the course. They'll thank the group. Thank the Lord, whatever, and I realise I helped. I made a difference. I'm validated. I know the theory, the best practices, the advice. Even if I can't stop smoking myself.

The first week is very boring. Jude, our coach, talks a lot. Ice breakers are met with horror. Old people reminisce about smoking in pubs and cafes. And cinemas. The coach gives advice about patches and pills and placebos. I have to sit through it all. That's my penance for coming back to group for the Christ-knows-how-many times.

They're all new faces. It's the usual eclectic mix; man in a wheelchair, woman straight from the office, broken-leg-and-crutches guy, pregnant woman. I'm the only repeat offender. Oh, and Beryl. Although I think she's lying about smoking.

And Hippy Girl. Hippy Girl arrives late. Her entrance is a ripple of floating purple. She's a vision of colour from her pink and purple dreadlocks and oversized shades (which she keeps on) to her flowery DMs, wafty skirt, crochet camisole top, and huge, peacock-feather earrings. I mean literally a fan of a tail in each ear. No, a whole peacock dangling from each lobe. And necklaces: a tiny vial on a leather thong, shells, beads, crystals, silver. Bangles crowd all the way up to her elbows on both arms, and she chink-chinks with every movement.

There is something about her. Not her presence, but something familiar.

She stinks of smoke.

'I know I stink of smoke,' she announces, 'I'm a shaman and I've come straight from a house cleansing. I've just walked through an entire five-bedroom house with a fistful of burning sage.'

We all stare at her, speechless. The group coach, embarrassed, rummages in her goody bag and fishes out the dextrose tablets before passing them around. Hippy Girl tugs gently on her dreads to adjust her wig, then catches me staring at her and smiles.

I snap my attention back to the coach. I feel the heat flush up my neck to my face. I don't know what I'm feeling but it's confusing.

That smile. Lascivious? Conspiratorial? Is she flirting? Or taking the piss? I'm sure I know her from somewhere, which makes it even worse.

I slip out of the room.

My Zippo is in my pocket. It helps me think. I rotate it, pushing with my thumb and flipping with my fingers, tracing the rough edges of the engraved initials. Over and over, I mould the smooth corners into my palm.

It's out of my pocket now. I like to flick the lid open and closed. The tiny metallic clang of the lid, as it springs back on the hinge, resonates on a frequency that settles my thoughts, hypnotises. Ping, click. Ping, click.

And the smell. Like catnip. Vaporous, dangerous, it makes my nostrils flare and my synapses snap. Ping, click.

The greased hinge leaves an oily residue on my fingers. I scrape my thumb over the cog, and the lighter sparks to life with a rasp of metal. I inhale the haze of fumes and watch the dancing yellow flame. Lights every time. No tricks, no knack, just a solid, loyal friend. In films, the pyro throws the Zippo into the pooling gasoline. Only a true bitch would throw their friend into the fire.

My heart beats hard in my throat. My thoughts race. My lips are dry, and I close my eyes to the sweet, chemical smell of the flame. I need fire. Now.

***

I put the battery back in the fire alarm and hide the galvanised bucket in the cupboard. It's not enough. It's like sniffing someone else's fag.

When I open my front door, the path shines after an all-night deluge. The leaking gutter plink-plinks on the lid of the wheelie bin. I wait at the kerb as cars sluice by, each one making a quick adjustment round The Pothole. It warrants capital letters in every email I have sent to the local council. It has become a phenomenon, a celebrity pothole.

As the traffic eases off, I can see that the flash of yellow is a rubber duck that someone has placed in the puddle in the hole. The duck wobbles and bobs, its smiling bill blissfully oblivious to its many scrapes with near annihilation. Last month, it had been a drowning Barbie Doll. Arms stretched up, one moulded boob poking out from the pink swimsuit. She eventually became wedged with just her feet above the water line.

Another car skids round the duck on its 'pond' and honks its horn at me. "It wasn't me," I think, although I wish it had been.

*

We're twenty minutes into week two of group. The new woman next to me has been shifting in her seat, a rolled-up towel in her lap. She raises her hand.

'Jenny, isn't it?' Coach puts on her best welcoming smile. As much as she likes the sound of her own voice, she does encourage participation.

'Yes. Erm. This isn't the hot yoga class, is it?' Poor Jenny has turned scarlet.

The group guffaws and giggles, and there are some lurid comments about what exactly "hot yoga" entails. Jenny apologises and scurries out of the room, bumping into a latecomer who takes up Jenny's empty chair.

A slick of glue glistens under her moustache as she settles into the seat. I try not to stare at him/her, but the left corner has lifted and twitches when he/she speaks. I am trying to be WOKE but it's her, Hippy Girl. Again. In another disguise. She has lowered her voice – to sound more manly.

'I have to keep my phone on during group. Sorry. I'm on call. This close to Guy Fawkes, you know...'

She's come as a firefighter. This should be good. She stinks like an old bonfire.

'I know I stink like an old bonfire,' she says with her gruff man voice, and embarks on a long and imaginative tale of a housefire she attended into the early hours. She gives elaborate details of the fire spreading, the house collapsing, the dark, the panic, the cries for help, the coughing. There are children and a kitten.

The group is rapt.

Her breathing equipment had failed, apparently. But she'd got them all out. She should still be at the hospital, but she'd discharged herself. Civilians. Her team. She's needed this time of year.

I still can't place her.

On cue, her phone rings. 'I'll be right there,' she says in her deep, throaty, male voice. She does a fake "Whadyaknow" shrug and leaves the group to thunderous applause.

Coach passes round the dextrose tablets – everyone needs a cigarette after that performance.

***

Today, The Pothole in my street has a miniature galleon floating on its puddle. Sails at full mast, it pitches and yaws with each passing vehicle. I don't know how long it's been there, but as I wait to cross the road, an articulated lorry crushes it to smithereens six times under each of its wheels. I assume that whoever put it there was aware that obliteration was a possibility. Shame really. it looked quite well made.

***

There's a punch up in the carpark after group. To be fair, tensions run high at week four. Week two, there's solidarity. Everyone has stopped smoking; they've made all their little changes. They're motivated. By the end of week three, no one has been near a smoking shelter, or a pub, and they've been asked a million times, 'How's it going?' accompanied by the universal sign for smoking a ciggie. Caffeine, nicotine, and normal life withdrawal has kicked in. Nerves are in shreds.

The old timer is surprisingly agile. He looks like he has some boxing experience, and three weeks of not smoking under his champion middle-weight belt means he's dancing around hoodie guy with considerable ease, his lungs now full of oxygen.

Hoodie guy is smarter than I gave him credit and holds up his hands in surrender. But then he punches the old timer square on the nose while the poor old thing is tucking his shirt tails in. Underhand. The crowd boos. And then we descend into a massive bundle, the likes of which I haven't seen since the school playground. Slapping, hair pulling and a lot of collar tugging. But no one goes over. We're all mindful of brittle bones and paper-thin skin.

The air is shattered by a high-pitched squeal. We all look up at Coach hanging out of the top window, puce with effort as she blows her rape whistle.

A chorus of repentant sinners sing out, 'Sorry, Jude.' The crowd separates with handshakes and back slaps. Dishevelled and red-faced but exhilarated, we disperse to our cars and cycles and the bus stop. I'm missing some hair. A packet passes from person to person. "They've caved," I think, but I'm relieved to see that it's a box of mints. I'm rather fond of this group. They have spirit.

After the group, I visit Dad, and the old feelings of revulsion at *his* lack of control, his inability to just damn well stop his own thing, make me feel physically sick. Everything about his place makes my bile rise. Literally.

Ammonia in the air stings my eyes. I pull the scarf up over my nose.

'Hi, Dad. Only me.'

'Come on through,' he calls from the kitchen at the rear of the house.

The beautiful parquet floor in the hall has long vanished under layers of old newspapers. The whole house has disappeared under piles of paper: bills, flyers, food labels. And cat shit. And cat sick. And crusted bowls, tins and plates of cat food. The cute bowls with cartoon fish on have disappeared under a mountain of crud. Any vessel that can hold kibble is fair game. A washing up bowl (he has no other use for it), saucers, Pirex dishes, Le Creuset pans, all filled to the top with dried cat food. Or full of stale water covered with a film of dust.

A decapitated and dismembered mouse is lying discarded on Mum's Persian rug. Its blue innards match the pattern, tonally.

Holding the takeaway coffees (see: washing up bowl) I pick my way through three tabbies, a black and white kitten with one eye, and a ginger tom nonchalantly licking its balls. My body thrums with a low rumble of purring, like when the train approaches on the underground.

The kitchen/diner had been my mother's pride and joy. *If she could see it now.* I cringe. Probably just as well she's gone off to Skegness with Colin from the King's Arms. That had been back when the cats were just a couple of fosters from the local rescue.

'I bought you a latte,' I say, manoeuvring the paper cup in between a pile of dirty paper plates and my dad's discarded dentures. He looks up from the crossword and gives me a gummy smile with genuine affection in those rheumy eyes.

'Thank you, love.'

Minnie, the white cat with pink, bald eyebrows, nudges Dad's cup as she high steps across the table. With a deftness that belies his frailty, Dad scoops her up and plonks her on his lap. His pink, puckered hands stroke her velvet pelt, the stiff, shrivelled fingers never moulding to the cat's shape. Minnie arches her back and pushes into the strokes.

'Good cat,' Dad says. 'Good cat.' He says it to all his cats, to any cat. It could be clawing his eyes out and shitting on his chin and he would say, 'Good cat.'

I don't think about the fire every time I look at my dad's scarred hands. Often, the memories take me by surprise, triggered by a smell or a sound. The distant tones of a police car, a freshly lit barbeque, the warmth of the oven on my face as I open the door. I'm there, standing barefoot in the grass, warm blades between my toes and tickling my ankles. The heat of our neighbour's inferno scorching my already sun-burned face.

For the millionth time, I watch my dad pound his fists on their door, screaming so hard his voice breaks like a teenager's. 'Wake up! Fire! Ben! Fliss! WAKE UP!'

And then Dad sitting in the back of the ambulance, his face sickly green behind the oxygen mask, flames dancing in his black hole eyes. His wrists balanced on his thighs, palms up, to keep the pressure off the glistening, pink, lamb cutlets that were his hands.

Behind me, the roar of water gushing out of the hose, and the moan and crack as their roof collapses. Dad asking, *did they find the dogs?* And the look on her face when I see Ben's daughter Fliss, sneak between the fire engines. How she raises her finger to her lips.

'Four sugars?' he checks.

'Yep. Four sugars.'

'There's a dead body in the hall. It stinks.'

'Hah! Seventeen down: carcass. Thanks, love.'

He scribbles the letters in the boxes while I look round the kitchen in despair. Dad's mattress sits in the dining area, dragged down from the bedroom, currently occupied by numerous curled up feline forms, licking, purring, and sleeping. More of them occupy his solitary armchair. He's cleared a path from the kitchen to the chair, but the full black sacks filled from that cleaning outburst, have been torn and rummaged, and their innards laid bare like the mouse's body.

I will find her. One day.

***

She's come as Anni-Frid from Abba. In a white jumpsuit.

'Sorry I'm late everyone. Been relocating a swarm.' She throws a veiled hat onto the empty seat beside her (no broken leg guy this week). She swats at an imaginary bee in front of her face, which elicits a high-pitched squeal from office tech guy.

He coughs, embarrassed. 'I'm allergic,' he says.

'It's gone.' Anni-Frid beams at the group. 'I'm extremely lucky because I'm totally immune to bee stings. And wasps. And hornets. Acidity in my skin or something. They won't come near me.' She's given herself freckles this week. And possibly false teeth; she's developed a lisp.

Anni stinks like a bonfire that's had water thrown on it.

'I probably stink like a bonfire,' she says. 'It's the smoker I use to calm my bees.' She is mesmerising. I wonder if she's tried snake-charming?

The coach has been giving out stress balls. We all sit there, squeezing lurid pink spheres. Coach says 'catch' to Anni-Frid and tosses a ball at her. Anni-Frid catches it with one hand and laughs.

I flinch at the image bursting into my mind.

I'm standing in the back garden with a wastepaper basket, and Fliss throws a tennis ball over the fence. I catch it in the basket with whoop. Before she can ask for it back, I yell, 'Catch,' and lob it over the boundary. She catches it in one raised hand, and lets out a surprised laugh.

Every muscle stiffens as I stare across the group circle. Anni-Frid is the neighbour's daughter. Anni-Frid is Fliss. Fliss has been coming to the group. My vision starts to tunnel, and my chest flares.

I have found her. No. She has found me.

Our eyes meet. She sees the recognition; she knows I know. She calls out, 'Catch!' and lobs the stress ball at me. Instinctively, I catch it with one hand. The group applauds. Fliss raises her finger to her lips.

***

I'm on the waste ground at the back of the toothpaste factory. The upturned crate digs into the backs of my thighs. I tried to keep the fire small, but it fans and shakes into the night sky, a shimmering phantasm. If someone sees it from the newbuilds, they'll call the fire service. I don't care.

My Zippo is still warm in my pocket as I turn it over, watching the flames. Noxious fumes seep into my scarf. There was something toxic in one of the barrels. I wanted an explosion. A big bang. Maybe even to get hurt with detonated debris. Or chemical burns.

But it's dying out now and filling the air with a charcoal smog, which makes my eyes water.

I stamp on the crate, furious with myself for letting her find me first. I kick the car door. Why hadn't I realised who she was? I drum my fists on the steering wheel because I've imagined this for so long.

***

I haven't seen Dad in a week. No, two. Shit.

She's the reason everything in my life is like it is:

Mum – gone. Getting married to Colin. Ugh.

Dad. The cats. The house. Ugh.

Me…My…Me. Ugh.

Oh Christ. Dad.

He'll be fine, of course. It's happened before: I go racing round there in a panic because, you know, life, and he's at the kitchen table doing the crossword with a jug of watered-down Carnation milk and some soft crackers. Not the end of the world. I'll do a shop at Waitrose (not at his request but to assuage my guilt) and I'll scrape the unidentifiable objects in his fridge into a black bag, which I'll bring home with me – see: many feral cats.

***

'Dad?'

I shove into the hallway, snow-ploughing flyers and post back against the wall. A herd of cats rushes at me. Rats out of a viaduct. Tails up, mewing pitifully, they stream down the stairs and plod through from the living room and kitchen. They run from the study and slink along the passage. There are scuffles as the more feral ones skitter for cover, bolting under boxes and behind the furniture.

'Dad, you there?' I shout over the cacophony of mewling. Something's not right. My heart is beating hard in my throat. I toe the cats out of my way, and they reseal the passageway behind me like an undammed river.

In the kitchen, I flick the light switch, but the bulb has gone. A tang of metal fills the air, along with the sweet nauseating stench of rotten meat. I think about putting the contents of Dad's fridge in a black bag and take it to the tip on the way home.

After stepping over cats and feeling along the surface, I pull up the blind, and an ochre wash fills up the kitchen.

My foot touches something, and I look down to see Dad on the floor. A skinny Siamese (he has a Siamese?) straddles his chest, sniffing at his face.

'Fuck off!'

It turns to look at me, with its tongue out, and a dreamy look, as though I've interrupted it. And I realise that's not its tongue but a piece of meat dangling from its mouth. The cat lets out a low growl and scarpers under the table.

'NO!'

My dad looks small and frail lying on the floor. His bones make tiny hills and vales in the crumpled landscape of his clothes. There's a dark patch at his crotch. *Oh Dad*

I spew my guts onto his tartan slippers.

When I look up, he stares back at me through milky eyes. Part of his nose is a ragged mess, and his lips have been pared back into a macabre grin. This is the first time I've seen him with his dentures in for months. I gag again. A tabby kitten ballet walks up his leg onto his chest. 'Fucksake.' I push it off his body and cover his face with a manky tea towel. All I can hear is my dad saying, 'Good cat,' with his new ventriloquist dummy mouth.

Something's going to burn.

***

I'm not first at group. A lone figure sits in the circle of chairs with her back to me. The hall door sucks air from the room as it closes, and she doesn't turn round. I take a seat a couple of chairs away from her. She looks up from the Zippo she's been turning over in her hands. I instinctively check my pocket and feel the cool edge of mine. We look at each other. Without a wig or facial hair or sunglasses, I can see the remnants of my childhood neighbour. Her close-together eyebrows and narrow shoulders.

'It's been a long time. I didn't recognise you the first couple of meetings,' I say.

She gives me one of her crooked smiles that I never could read, and looks down at the Zippo, flipping it over. My stomach flips with it – I know exactly how it feels: the texture, the weight of it. She doesn't look up from it when she speaks.

'It's a terrible burden when your own birth is a matricide. But it's a greater burden still, to bear the utter barren sadness of a grieving father.'

I swallow hard, my throat already dry. I can feel the warm skin of her neck. The click and nudge of cartilage under my thumbs. A speck of spittle lands on my cheek as she gasps and splutters.

I'm holding my breath. This is just one of many ways I've imagined ending her.

'I know,' she says, mistaking my silence for second-hand embarrassment, 'too much information. But those were the starting blocks of my life – mother gone and a sad father.' She gives a little half-smile that forms a straight-line dimple from her chin to her eye crease.

I might explode with the bitterness of my empathy. How can she be the only person I've ever met that gets the loss, the desolation of living with a father's despair? Especially as it's all her fault. All of it. Every crack and fissure. Every tectonic shift. I want to embrace her until she can't breathe.

It's then I notice Fliss's blue jumper with the ink stain on the right cuff. Like mine. And the black ankle boots with two straps and buckles. Like mine. She has a fringe and a ponytail. And the Zippo. Tonight, she's come as me.

I punch her in the face. Her teeth snap, and her lips make a strange slapping sound. She's shifted on her chair, and she gasps and groans. I shove her onto the floor and pick up the chair, smashing it down on her back and head. I don't know if it's the splinter of wood or bone, but I keep going. Smash. Lift. Crash. Lift. They might be my grunts; they might be hers. Bits of wood fly out until all that remains is a chair leg with a spur of the broken seat. I am holding it over my head, heaving in and out breaths, looking at her curled in a ball with a battered head and arms. She has stopped moving. There are little gurgles, so I know she's still breathing.

I drop the chair.

Now, I move like a dancer. I step over her and pull the remaining wooden chairs into a pile. There's a box of craft stuff in the corner of the hall that belongs to the WI. I grab out some tissue and crepe paper and stuff it between the legs. In my bag is the yellow tin of light fluid for my Zippo. I empty it onto the paper and the chairs. I need more kindling.

The tiny kitchen stinks of old washing up cloths and bleach. Under the sink is a pile of old newspapers in a wooden crate. I drag it through to the hall and dress the pyre.

My Zippo is in my hand. I light one of the newspapers and step back as it whooshes to life. Fliss is still unconscious, her legs close to the pile of chairs. I linger in the open door to watch the flames as they smoke and climb. The smell is intoxicating. I breathe it in and then close the door and turn the key in the lock.

I shouldn't be surprised at how quickly the old scout hut burns.

I don't know how long I've been hypnotised by the fire when I hear Jude shouting into her mobile for a fire engine. The group have arrived and gathered in a huddle round her.

Beryl comes to stand beside me. She's cracked and shrivelled like an old leather handbag. Another regular like me, she couldn't get to the first couple of meetings because of her emphysema. Beryl always stops smoking. She starts again and comes back to the group when she's lonely.

'Where's the mystery shopper girl?' She frowns.

'Who?' I cough.

'You know, the funny girl with all the silly disguises. She must be a mystery shopper or an auditor or something.'

Beryl looks to the group and then back at me.

'Or maybe she just needs to get some help really?'

SHIT.

I stare at the snaking flames and nurse my throbbing knuckles. The wooden structure screams and squeaks. Then the wind changes direction and envelops our small group in choking ash. We all back up, coughing and covering our faces.

On the grass verge, with the orange and pink haze of the fire lighting up the dusk sky, I'm back on my neighbour's lawn.

The distant wail of a fire truck sounds like my dad's broken voice, screaming out to Ben and his daughter as he pounds on the door trying to save them.

So here I am. Staring at the scout hut.

Oh Christ.

I pull away from the group and run to the door hearing shouts of disbelief behind me. With my jumper pulled over my fingers, I twist the key in the lock, the heat of the blaze scorching my face and fingers. It won't budge. I kick and kick at the door, feeling the wood buckle as the pain jolts through my knee. It splinters, and I kick again as a blast of hot air knocks me backwards. I right myself, and with my arms up at my face, I charge through the opening.

Fliss has moved. She's right by the door like I imagined. Something clamps on my shoulder. The roof must have collapsed. I'm being dragged backwards. I feel the change to the cold air of the night. Big, cumbersome figures lumber past me and grab Fliss and pull her to the door and outside.

The shouts are barely audible over the gush of water and the churn of the engine. Someone's holding my face and asking me questions.

'I'm fine,' I say, 'I'm fine.'

Fliss is heaved onto a gurney, an oxygen mask pushed into her face. She coughs and tries to sit up. I sigh, relieved she's alive.

I glance over to the pavement. My group are still huddled together. Beryl raises her thumb and nods. Someone passes round a pack of Silk Cut. They stand in a tight circle, taking soothing inhalations of smoke before letting out a collective huff of relief. I look at the guilty faces. The relieved faces. The agonised and the resigned faces. They'll be fine. Plenty to talk about next time.

Then I look down. A paramedic kneels in front of me and examines my hands with a tenderness that makes me burst into tears. Salty splashes land on my tattered, singed palms, but they're too burned to hurt.

Yet.

***

It's difficult wielding a trowel with bandaged hands but it's 2am in the morning and I'm driven by the madness of insomnia. The Pothole has dried out now, and I pack it with some hardcore and my Zippo, then the dregs of a bag of compost. I poke a hole with the blunt end of the trowel and place the marigold seedling on top. The council have put an orange barrier round The Pothole, pending repair. A bit like Fliss.

She took the blame for the fire. My fire. Not hers. But the outcome is the same, I suppose. She's getting the help she needs. And I'm not a murderer.

I hope the barrier is there long enough for the flower to grow.

Man-eater

It was the summer of death.

The girls stood on the dry, cracked riverbank. The strip of mud had doubled in size and looked like a jigsaw puzzle. What was left of the river scrabbled at the edges like a thirsty hound.

Daisy shielded her eyes and squinted into the cloudless blue sky. The azure wash spread as far as the eye could see, and the sun blazed white as it beat down on their heads. Vultures rode on the thermals, tiny specks circling high until they disappeared, evaporated by the heat.

Daisy kicked impatiently at a lump of dirt.

'Keep still, Dais.' Clementine tugged on her hair like their Mama did when she braided. Daisy passed the yellow ribbon to her sister and after another tug, Clem squeezed her shoulders, just like Mama, to show she was all finished.

Daisy didn't get how Clem managed to keep so shipshape all day; her hair never needed braiding again. Daisy wiped the sweat off her face with the hem of her dress and shooed the flies away.

'Let's go see the hornets' nest in John Adams' maple,' said Clem. She picked up her broken corn stalk and swished it like a sword.

Daisy shrugged her silent protest and followed a lizard as it wiggled into the undergrowth. Clem poked at the ground with her stick. Bits of it broke off in the hollows of dried claw prints.

They stood and watched the river awhile. It ran fast through the middle, the currents even more unpredictable now the brown waters were forced through the gaps like tobacco juice through stained teeth.

'I miss Old Todd.'

Daisy had said this at least once a day since he'd passed earlier that summer.

'Jeez,' said Clem, and Daisy's eyes widened at her sister's cuss.

Old Todd had died of heatstroke early on, in what would be the hottest summer in recorded history. The ground was so hard, Daddy couldn't dig him a grave. Instead, they to put Old Todd out with the trash.

'That's no burial for a god-fearing dog,' she wailed. Mama took her frustration out on the dishes and said that Old Todd wouldn't mind one bit since he'd spent most of his life with his nose in the trash.

Daisy asked Mama if they put Mr Smithson out with the trash when he died. Mama realised her mistake too late when she mentioned the special digger at the church. Daisy was inconsolable when she heard that, *'no they couldn't take Old Todd to the graveyard, and no, the church wouldn't let Daddy borrow the special digger to bury her dog.'*

After the garbage truck had rumbled down the track with Daisy running behind it, she'd wept for three, long days straight refusing to come out of her room.

The buzz and rattle of the cicadas was electric in the air. Heat shimmered over the scrubland. John Adams' barn wobbled like Jell-O in the distance. His corn was long finished, but a few lone stalks stood like scarecrows, their brown cob silks hanging limp against their tinder-dry husks.

Daisy chewed at her fingernails and stared hard at the opposite bank. Something long and grey floated half-submerged and bumped lazily against the outstretched fingers of the mangroves. Clem followed her stare.

'Gator,' Clem said, and her little sister took a step back from the edge. Daisy bit into her cuticles. Without taking her eyes off the water, Clem reached over and moved Daisy's hand away from her mouth.

'It's a biggun.'

Daisy chewed the nails on her other hand.

Three huge boulders at the foot of the other bank pushed the flow towards the girls. When the river was full, every now and then something interesting would wash up on the sliver of beach. The girls had found a tennis sock, the arm of a doll with painted tattoos, and a top set of dentures. One time, a bottle full of mustard coloured liquid washed up. Clem had kicked it back in the river, saying it looked like the devil's work. But Clem always said that when she didn't know how to explain something.

The floating lump was the colour of corn smut and bloated like a puffer fish. It drifted to their feet and slapped in the wet gravel. A sickly stench rose from the mud, so foul they pulled their dress collars over their faces.

'The gator's wearing Patty-Mae's sweater,' said Daisy. Although wet and filthy, and stretched to bursting over the swollen flesh, Patty-Mae Adams' leopard-print top with the plunging neckline and black, satin trim, was unmistakable.

'That ain't no gator,' Clem said and raised the corn stalk to poke at the bloated corpse.

'Don't,' said Daisy. She fidgeted from foot to foot.

'We better go tell Daddy.' Clem grabbed Daisy's hand, pulled her up the bank and marched off towards the parched fields, dragging her little sister behind.

'I'm glad Patty-Mae's gone,' said Daisy, trying to twist free from her sister's grip.

Clem swung her round and whispered in her face, 'Why would you say such a thing?'

'Cos I heard Mama and Patty-Mae shouting and cursing, and after, Mama said to me you stay away from that Patty-Mae Adams, she's a man-eater.'

Clem pursed her lips and shook her head. She had that look on her face Daisy had seen in class. She didn't understand either, but she was trying to look like she knew.

A cloud of midges performed its tiny murmuration between their heads. Clem flapped at them. They dispersed and regrouped like mercury. The girls blew them away and set off through John Adams' field.

Clem put her arm through Daisy's. Picking a path through the stubble, they kicked stones and toed the shrivelled cobs. The corn stalks had wilted and collapsed. There was plenty of gossip in town about why Mr Adams had planted so late in the season. Some folk said it wasn't just his crop that was ruined.

On the horizon, a bruised cloud reached its thick-set fingers round the mountain peaks.

The girls balanced on rock-hard ridges and swiped at each other with their sticks, creating dust clouds that made them cough and screw up their eyes.

'Reverend Jedediah's gonna need his special digger again,' said Daisy. She tossed the stalk away and let out a noisy sigh.

'I miss Old Todd.'

Okay. You Can Have My Kidneys

Day 78

Noah missed her. She'd been his filter, his carer. Until she hadn't. He stood in the doorway of his apartment, and various alarms and reminders flashed and bleeped from his house tablet. He punched in the code and cleared all the warnings that the milk was off in the fridge, and his sink tap had a leak.

The rooms were cold and dust-filled. The robo-cleaner sat at a weird angle on its plinth, uncharged. Everything was drained of charge, of life, of energy. He stepped on the bin pedal and dropped in a dead plant along with the solid carton of milk from the fridge.

His nanites were busy rebuilding his liver. They couldn't help with the space left beside him. He held on to the counter, afraid he might float up to the ceiling without his anchor. Without Esther.

He checked his wrist display.

Okay. You can have my kidneys 😉

The last message he'd sent her blinked, unread.

Day 75

'I can't believe it, twinny.'

Just like that, the consultant was ready to operate, after nearly three months wait. Seventy-five days attached to each other, right side, to right side. Conjoined. Twins. Half their shared liver each, a shedload of reprogrammed nanites and the operation scheduled for two hours' time. They'd have to sort out with legal about finances etc, etc.

They were both drowsy on pre-meds. A gentle Rumba played through the room speakers, and they were having a last dance. Noah stumbled a couple of times, but his technique was much improved.

'Will you still dance afterwards?' She rested her heavy head on his shoulder.

'You know, I might,' he said, and twirled them both round in a fancy flourish. 'Will you still read? Books, I mean.'

'Maybe...

What's the first thing you'll do when you get out of here?' she asked.

He didn't miss a beat. 'Go to the gym.'

'What about your job?'

'Oh yeah. That, and go to the gym.'

They laughed.

She closed her eyes and sighed. 'I'm going to have a bath. A really hot, deep bath and a huge glass of fizz. And sleep on my stomach. I am so done with sleeping stood up.'

The clocked ticked. The medbot hummed in its charger. The air conditioning hissed.

'Will we...will I see you again?'

Day 44

The moon was shining high and bright in the evening sky. They could leave the blinds open these days. The paparazzi had lost interest in them after a major celebrity had come out as a hamster.

There was a palpable change to the energy between them since the sex thing. A loss of tension. An easy existence between them. Easier.

Some days, she buried her face in the pillow and screamed until she was hoarse. Usually after the consultant had left. She ranted, 'Stupid man in his stupid matching waistcoat and bowtie. Stupid platitudes. He'd say (in a wheedling, snippy voice), "We understand how difficult this must be, but we need to run just a few more tests to be absolutely certain we can operate a risk-free separation, blah, blah, blah."'

Noah stayed quiet. He'd learned the patterns of her anger. The rant. The tears. The mock lull, the false silence. He knew not to interrupt, to let her see these emotions through to the bitter end. Either a voice-breaking tirade or the half sentence of utter despair.

'They're delaying this on purpose,' she croaked, her throat wrecked by the scream. 'They just want to study us. We're Guinea pigs. A freak show. Two organs to be poked and prodded and filmed.'

He tried. 'I think they're being careful. I want to come out of this alive, don't you?'

She shook her head. 'I don't even care. I'm so done with this. With us.'

And even the offer of a quick tango didn't cheer her up. Esther asked to go to bed early. Noah conceded like he always did. He kept his arms to himself. Esther needed her space.

Day 28

They danced most mornings. The treadmill had been a disaster. Weights were unworkable. Walking was tedious; someone was always going backwards. But dancing was fun. Esther was a good teacher. She'd had classes as a child. She loved to dance; it was obvious. With the steps adapted to their unusual position and simplified for Noah, they swayed. The waltz, rumba, cha-cha. And they laughed. Often.

The connective skin between them had stretched and strengthened, so movement was a lot less painful. Now, they were attached from ribs to hip. The doctors assured them this would not hinder the progress into their separation, but the prognosis remained oblique. And often just bleak. But Noah didn't say that.

They showered together now. No chaperone, no clingy shower curtain. They peed together too, and the rest. All the modesty and hiding were time consuming and exhausting. They were two human beings doing what was natural. They knew each other's bodies, habits and quirks. With this freedom came a different sort of dignity.

'Could you masturbate more quietly?'

'Fuck!'

'We could, help each other out? You know, like friends with benefits. We do everything else together.'

Day 15

'1, 2, 3, 2, 2, 3, 3, 2, 3, 4, 2, 3, and left foot back. 1, 2, 3....'

Noah was finally relaxing into the dance. He held her waist with a feather touch and rested his other hand on her shoulder. She had to lead him most of the time. She giggled.

'What did I do?' he said and stopped.

'Nothing, it's just, we really need to get you leading. Or you'll be on a dance floor treading on some poor girl's toes.'

He frowned. 'I don't see me ever doing this with anyone else.'

In the silence that followed, Esther wondered at the multiple meanings of that statement. The thought that they might be stuck together like this forever. Or move the emphasis from *this* to *anyone*, and there was a hint of a possible future. She shook the thought out of her head and moved to pull away, forgetting for a moment, that she couldn't.

'Had enough?'

'Yeah. Let's sit for a bit.'

'Do you think they're any closer to separating us?' She chewed on a thumbnail.

He shrugged. 'Absolutely. It'll be fine. Don't crack up on me.'

'Hmmm.'

'I'm going to read my book.'

'Yeah, why not, me too.'

At the end of the chapter, Esther looked at Noah. He had a little groove in his forehead when he concentrated. She hadn't heard him laugh out loud at a book, but sometimes the corner of his mouth twitched in amusement. Sometimes, it even twitched to something she'd said. She closed the book, slung it on the side table.

Day 10

Noah woke exhausted. Neither of them could get comfortable sleeping vertically, strapped to a mattress. But, on a normal bed, someone was always face down, and someone always tried to turn over in the night. The vertical beds worked better. 'Just like in the space station,' the nurse had quipped to twin glares.

Noah turned his head to look at Esther. She slept, face towards him, her lips slightly parted. He could feel her breath on his nose. The nanites had fixed the broken vessels in her cheeks, and the dark circles under her eyes. Without all the raised eyebrow nonchalance and sneering bravado, she was beautiful. Through the blinds, the strips of sunlight highlighted the fine down on her face. He reached out to stroke her cheek.

***

Esther woke to Noah raising his hand to touch her face. The look in his eyes was so tender and protective, she forgot herself and smiled sleepily at him. He dropped his hand and said, 'Day ten.'

'Morning, twinny.' She stretched, trying not too hard to miss his head. She knew how much it irritated him.

'I need to pee,' she said.

'Me too.'

'Do you have your own kidneys?'

'Hands off, Esther, like I'd ever let that happen again?'

The medbot left its charging point and released the sleep straps. They did their sideways shuffle to get free from the vertical beds.

It was their habit now to walk round the axis of each other to stretch their legs. Then they took it in turns to walk backwards.

Day 1

The last of the team of white coats closed the door behind them. The medbot whirred into action checking vitals for both patients. It glided round them, tightening the straps on their respective vertical med beds. Then it wheeled back into its charging point and hummed on standby.

Esther blew out, ruffling her fringe. She smacked her lips and made popping sounds.

'So, thanks for the liver.'

He rolled his eyes. 'What the liver you tried to destroy last night?'

'I wasn't destroying it – just putting it through its paces.'

'You could have died, the amount of shit you...ingested.'

'Don't get all judgy on me. I didn't sell a perfectly good organ for 190,000 credits.'

'180,500. I forfeited five percent because you agreed you would leave the District. So that this didn't happen.' He gestured to their conjoined bodies.

'Ah.'

'Did you even read the contract?'

'Kinda...'

Esther was distracted by the flecks of spit that had landed on her cheek. Their bodies were so close. She didn't wipe her face. Noah looked furious.

'I was hoping for a hangover from hell today. And my winnings from the game.' She flicked her wrist and checked her credit balance on the display. 'Bummed out on both accounts.'

Noah checked his wrist. 'And I was hoping not to be fused in some weird DNA-nanite-fuck up this morning. Also, I'm missing the merger meeting at work. I might not even have a job by the time we're done here. So, thanks for that.'

'Wow. Chill the fuck out. Not my fault. If they were going to lose you after one meeting, then maybe the company's shit anyway? Who is it?'

'Travis and Proctor.'

'Oh, that's my uncle. He's Travis. I can ask him...'

'...No! Stay out of my business.'

'Fine.' She rolled her eyes.

The medbot whirred into action.

Heart rates elevated. Patients will remain calm. Nanites unable to comply at this time. Recommend 20mg Diazepam.

'No, thank you!'

'Yes! About time.'

They glared at each other. The medbot sparked, fizzed and slumped over in a tangle of metal.

'Oops.'

Day Zero

Noah leaned on the bar and watched the strobe lights dance across heads. The basey beat vibrated through his whole body, a superimposed heartbeat to challenge his own. From their table, his friends grabbed the drinks from the waitress he'd sent over. A couple of them caught his eye and gave him a thumbs up. He was being generous tonight. His student loans were paid off. His apprentice advance from five years ago was cleared. He'd even paid off his school loan for his parents. He had a clean slate. He felt emancipated.

Shouts and applause rose up from the corner. Noah looked over. In the private sector, cordoned off with sheer curtains, a group of glitterati whooped and laughed. They hugged close and shook hands, careful to touch wrist to wrist, to pass over or receive payment. They were obviously playing Beat Ya Nan.

Beat Ya Nan is not a game of grandparent-directed violence, but a gamble to get as many narcotics and booze into your system before your nanites stop the hit. It's all about the highs. How intense, how long. It's a betting game, too. The first person whose nanites kick in, loses.

Noah pushed off from the bar and squeezed through the crush. At the cordon, he bumped his way through the spectators to watch the game.

Over the centre table, a huge, mirrored ball turned, reflecting light on pearly teeth and sequined dresses. The hoppy, sour stench of strong alcohol made Noah's head spin like the disco ball. On the table, crates of champagne and spirits were being opened and passed round the gamers. They tilted back their heads and glugged mouthful after mouthful of drink. Other contestants snorted, injected or ingested scooped handfuls of powders, in every shade of decadence. The air around them was filled with dust motes, a cocktail of coke and meth and speed. Noah's fellow spectators took great gulps of air, inhaling the free hits. Noah smiled to himself, smug in the knowledge he currently had enough credit to join the game.

The amount of credit needed to fund this habit was phenomenal and therefore only accessible to the glitterati and their bottomless trust funds. Even though Noah had the funds now, it had always struck him as an inordinate waste of credit. And everyone remembered the KT Spence disaster, when the rapper's nanites had glitched at the overload and left him with his eyeballs exploding as he choked on his own vomit.

Noah took a long deep lungful of the drug-fuelled air. Before his nanites set to work dispelling the drugs from his system, there was a moment of total silence. All around him, the faces and bodies swirled and swam as if they were paints on a canvas. He moved his hands in front of his body, merging their faces with his fingers. He lifted from the floor; his lungs filled with so much love and joy it was going to take him to the ceiling.

And then he felt the concrete beneath him, and his vision cleared. He was cleansed.

A roar of 'WOAH!' rose from the glitterati. A gorgeous girl in a tiny green dress was chugging a litre of tequila. Her head tilted back, and her slim throat pulsated with every gulp. She finished the bottle, slammed it on the table, and grabbed a jet injector before plunging it into her neck, narrowly missing her toxin sensor. Then she pushed her face into a mound of white powder and lifted her head snorting and coughing and sneezing. Her cohort screamed in disbelief.

The girl stumbled towards the crowd, yanking down the drapes as she tried to stay upright. Her eyes were bloodshot, and one rolled to the back of her head. Her nose was bleeding. She moaned and clawed at her white-powdered face, now in obvious distress.

Noah grunted as the girl crashed into him. The sensor on her neck still blinked green. She needed a MedBot.

'No MedBots – just get me outside.'

'Hey!' Behind him, Noah saw the referee spread his hands and jut out his jaw. With the girl draped across his shoulder, Noah led her to the neon pink exit sign, pushed against the bar on the door, and they tumbled into the cool night air. The girl threw up over his shoes.

'That's bett...' she threw up again. And again. Finally, she dry-retched and straightened up, walking her hands up her legs.

'I think I'm gonna fain...'

He caught her as she careened forwards. An intense stabbing pain shot through his right side, as if something was trying to cut its way out.

'What the fuck?'

The girl had her arms loosely hung round his neck, but she was pressed so close to him, her head lolled on his shoulder.

He thought maybe he'd become impaled on something the girl had on her. They were wedged right side to right side in a macabre dance hold. His freshly healed scar was pulsing with pain. But it was the area just above it that felt like it had split in two.

I'm dying.

Noah was falling. The girl's arms flailed out to her sides like wings, but their bodies stayed locked. Her hair smelled of apples. He blacked out.

The week before

In a medical facility in the BetaMedCore district, Esther drifted back to consciousness. When she opened her eyes, a MedBot and a nurse were already dialling up her pain meds. She sighed as a warm sensation started in her head and dribbled down her face, like a hot oil treatment. The tingle spread through her neck and shoulders and trickled down her spine. She trembled.

'Are you cold?' the nurse asked.

'No. Nanites are kicking in, that's all.'

'Erm, the nanites are on hold while your new organ stabilises – that's the pain medication starting to work. Remember, Dr Johns explained that there would be a four-week recovery period?'

Esther laid back with a smile and closed her eyes. This is why she had paid for a new liver: four whole weeks of real-time highs (and lows), four weeks of her body and brain having a nanite-free response to drugs, drink and adrenaline. Four weeks of the 'au naturel' response to uppers, kickers, stardust, and dope.

She sat up and groaned as her muscles screamed, and the wound tightened.

'How soon can I be discharged?'

***

A few blocks away, in the Delta District Clinic, Noah slid his legs over the side of the bed and planted his bare feet on the ground. The tiles were cold. He stood up, moving the drip tube back over his shoulder.

When he lifted his hospital gown, there was a stiffness to his right side. And the tiniest mark under his lowest rib. An insect bite. The smallest incision. But no bruising yet. And, of course, the much longer purple scar where they'd removed his liver. The nanites had been busy healing.

Despite the extensive use of Nanorgans, harvested organs 'au naturel' were still highly sort after. As part of his contract, Noah had relinquished all rights to the 'aforementioned organ'.

By way of recompense, it had been replaced with the very latest Adult Liver Ver 7.4. His credit balance was now several zeros in the black. A hefty investment into his future.

Walking to look out of the small grill window, he felt lighter. Lopsided. Empty on one side. Emptier.

Can you miss an organ? Something that exists, despite you? That filters for you, cares for you. Until it doesn't. Can you miss that organ? Noah did.

Content Warnings

What's New, Kitty Kat?

An amputee copes with abandonment and disability. Sexual references.

Mightier

Set in Early 20th century. Contains sexual violence references and violence.

Buried Alive

Set in a theme park this story has references to addictions, debt, disfigurement, body horror, and contains violence.

The Restoration Man

Gothic story contains taxidermy.

Talking in Tongues

A story about cult survivors. Violence, child abuse, mental health.

Strange Honeymoon

Steam punk/fantasy set in a circus. Domestic violence references, violence, addiction, body horror.

Thin Places

Sci-fi set in a future with sophisticated VR weight loss programmes. Contains bodily fluids, choking, obesity, loss.

Hunt

Contains violence, animal violence, and loss.

Sister

This story explores bereavement, grief, abandonment. It contains suicide ideation, self-harm and mental health.

Smoke

A member of a stop smoking group battles with addiction, hoarding, animal abuse, grief, impulse-control-disorder. Contains violence.

Man-eater

Two sisters play in their backyard in the deep south. Loss and death.

Okay. You Can Have My Kidneys

Nanopunk set in a future where organs are sold and replaced for credits. Sexual references, body horror, self-harm, addiction, drug use.

About the Author

Jessica Joy has stories in several anthologies, including *Graduation* in 'With Our Eyes Open,' *Russian Doll* in 'Transforming Being' – Bridge House Publishing; *Fracture Clinic* in The Rabbit Hole 2 – The Writers Co-op; *Forecourt Flowers* in The Tyranny of Bacon – Pure Slush Books; and *Alabama Rot* in Love & Life Eternal (Amazon).
She won the Faber Academy QuickFic competition with *Peach* and was runner up with *Buoyant*.

Canterbury Christchurch University, who've awarded Jessica a Creative Writing MA with Distinction, have published two of her short stories, along with a collaborative poem.

When she's not writing, Jessica enjoys running and planning her escape.

Bluesky @j-essjoy.bsky.social
X @MrsJessicaJoy1
Instagram and Threads @jessica.joy83

Printed in Dunstable, United Kingdom